HARPO'S GARDEN

and other stories

Also by Roger Lee Kenvin

After the Silver Age

The Cantabrigian Rowing Society's Saturday Night
Bash

The Gaffer and Seven Fables

Krishnalight

HARPO'S GARDEN

and other stories

by

Roger Lee Kenvin

JULY BLUE PRESS

Published by *July Blue Press*, 126 Mt. Cardigan Road, Alexandria, New Hampshire 03222.

First printing 1997
Second printing 1998

Printed in the United States of America by Odyssey Press Inc., Dover, New Hampshire

Library of Congress Catalog Card Number: 97-93024

ISBN 0-9656635-3-1

ACKNOWLEDGMENT

"The Sound of Snow Falling" and "Harpo's Garden" (as "Counterpane") originally appeared in *Roanoke Review*; "China" in *The Monocacy Valley Review*; "Starfish" in *Potpourri*; "The Eye of the Piano" in *The South Carolina Review*; "Harpo Inamorato" *in Soundings East*; "Sumner of the Spanish Main" in *Mostly Maine*; "Austria Noon" in *The Writing on the Wall*; and "The Winds of March" in *Kennebec: A Journal of Maine Writing*.

For Rudd

"Gone from the map the shore where childhood played,
Tight-fisted as a peasant, eating love."

W. H. Auden

TABLE OF CONTENTS

HARPO'S GARDEN

I am in the hospital recovering from a serious disc operation. The fifth lumbar. I wrecked it in a dangerous skiing accident. They had to have both an orthopedic surgeon and a neurosurgeon in on the job. So I am lying here in my hospital bed, wondering if I'm going to make it, receiving healthy shots of demerol every four hours and hallucinating pleasantly. It is 3:00 a.m., but what the hell. I ring for the nurse. She should see what I just saw. Outside my hospital window, illuminated by the bright moon, a cloud just passed by in the shape of Harpo Marx. He tipped his hat and smiled at me that mysterious enigmatic Harpo smile as he sailed by.

"Try to sleep," says the nurse, transferring a Renoir bouquet of flowers from the table to the window sill.

"I am trying," I say. But I can't sleep. Sometimes medication works the other way on me. Give me something to make me sleep, I'll stay awake for hours. Hype me up, I'll fall off to sleep.

I focus on the flowers, but I am thinking about another Harpo right now. My brother, little Harpo. I am eight years old and he is a baby about nine months old. I am wheeling him in his stroller on the roadside in front of our house in Maine. I am allowed to do that. Harpo has a big mop of curly blond hair. He has bright blue eyes and smiles at everybody. "Harpo is a smiler," I say to everyone who stops to admire him.

I meet two boys around ten and eleven who live down the block. "Is that a girl?" one of them asks.

"No, it's a boy," I say. I don't like these guys. They have nothing better to do than run around on other people's property and pick fights with younger kids like me.

"Looks like a little girl," says Stan, the older, meaner one. Andy, the other, laughs like a hyena.

"Let us get by," I say. They are blocking the way.

"Turn around, stupid," Stan says. "Take that little monkey girl back home."

I turn the stroller around. Harpo smiles and bats his arms on the side.

"Wipe that stupid smile off your face," says Stan. I move Harpo out of that enemy territory fast. We head toward home.

I am fifteen. I am lifting weights in the garage to build up my biceps and triceps. I do this every day after school for half an hour. I want to be on the wrestling team. Nobody else is home yet.

I hear a crying noise. I hear the back door near the garage open. The crying noise stops. I put down my weights, wondering what has happened. I go into the house. Harpo is in the kitchen crying.

"What happened?" Harpo is shaking and blubbering.

"Miss Davis hit me." He holds out his hands.

I see red. "Where? Why?"

"Here." Pathetic little hands trembling in front of me. "With her ruler."

"What for?"

A direct look into my eyes. "I left the seat up."

"She'll pay for this," I say. "Wait here. Get a glass of water." I storm out of the house. I march the mile and a half to school, cutting over people's lawns, not smiling, not saying hello to people I know. I am determined to humiliate Miss Davis for what she did to my brother.

I storm down the hall of the school. Miss Davis is not in her room. She is in a windowless room with the principal, other teachers, and a lot of bad air. I can see all of them through the partially opened door. I race down the hall again and surprise the janitor in his closet. "Where is the key to that teachers' conference room?" I demand. Astonished, he indicates a key hanging on a nail. There is a tag reading "Tchrs. Conf." dripping down from it. Before he can do anything about it, I grab the key and run down the hall, thrusting the key into the lock and slamming the door shut. I lock all the enemies into one air-tight cube in which all are doomed to die. Through the little jail-like window in the door, I can see a bunch of angry teachers rising up, wondering what in hell is going on. "You're locked in, you bitch," I shout. "Child hater, child hater!" I dash out the front door of the school and throw the key into a bush. I don't care if they arrest me. I don't care if they capture me and kill me. Nobody does that to my brother. Harpo never hurt anybody or anything in his life.

There are great dark windswept pines all around our house. We lived right in the middle of the forest when we first moved here. Gradually, the forest was sold little by little, mostly to summer people, and houses went up all around us. Every day the forest gets smaller and smaller. Still, there are pines, supple sassafras trees, and the remains of an apple orchard for a boy to climb up in and build tree houses.
"You may climb in any tree around except the pines," said my mother. "Pines have thin branches and are dangerous. You could fall out of them."
I listened and I never climbed a pine tree. Jenny listened and she never climbed a pine either. Harpo listened, but one Sunday climbed one. The branch broke under him, sending him quite a distance to the ground. The wind was knocked clear out of him. He couldn't speak. He lay on the ground panting for air. We ran and got my mother. "Harpo's dead," screamed Jenny. My mother came fast. She took in the whole scene quickly. She stood patiently over Harpo until his little body began quivering with life again. "Why did you climb that tree?" asked my mother. "I told you that you could have a bad fall."

"A bird kicked me," said Harpo, smiling his little smile at Mother. Jenny and I hooted with laughter. We thought Harpo was inventive and original. Mother said he wasn't, he simply was a born hooligan. But I noticed she grinned with a secret delight when she said it.

Harpo is going to college. Jenny and I have been there and back. Naturally, we know everything. We fuss over Harpo. Does he have this? Does he have that? "You will need a clipboard, Harpo. Do you know what courses you will take? You will need to budget your money for your books. Think before you join any fraternity. Be sure to look up Professor Daniels. Tell him you are my brother. He will remember me. Write once a week. Call when you get there. When you reach the dorm and get settled, phone right away so we can get all your impressions."

Six hours minimum. That's how long the trip will take the fastest driver across New England from Port Clyde to Portland to North Conway to Woodsville and then down route 10 to Hanover. It's cold there. It could be snowing even now. Harpo's ride is almost two hours late in arriving. Harpo doesn't really know Tom Aylwen who is driving down from Bar Harbor. Tom is a junior at Dartmouth and will be Harpo's Big Brother. I can see that Harpo is disappointed that Tom is late. Harpo looks at me. I know he's thinking that I wouldn't be late for such an important event in his life.

It is almost 3:00 p.m. Harpo is worn out. His eyes are red with anxiety and lack of sleep last night. He has two large L. L. Bean duffels, both bulging at the seams. Finally, Tom arrives. He has a mustache, longish hair, and smokes. He tells Harpo his father was late in getting the car back to him that morning. I can sense that Harpo is relieved to see that Tom is not a spoiled rich kid. Harpo jumps into the car and looks more relaxed now. Tom says they will pick up another passenger in Portland and another somewhere in the White Mountains near Crawford Notch. Tom's silver Buick pulls away. We all wave furiously. "Goodbye, Harpo. Good luck.

You will love it, I know," shouts out Jenny like a deranged cheerleader. My mother's face says the opposite. I put my arm around her protectively. But my spine suddenly shivers involuntarily. I am worried about Harpo. That silver Buick disappeared too easily down the road.

You go off to college in 1968 as a promising freshman. When it doesn't work out and your grades slide, your whole soul and being starts slipping too. And so you come back from a war, instead of college, a few years later as an imperfect, damaged man. Something nasty hanging in the sky over you moves you around, slides you into position to be a little piece in the unpopular game called "Viet Nam." It's just like Tag: You are "it." The object is to get home free. If you can do it, that's all that matters.

I never saw Harpo again until he came home. He did luck out with only a severe leg wound that healed miraculously, but he no longer smiled. He finished his last two years at Dartmouth in almost mechanical fashion, majoring in chemistry. "Making bombs, Patrick," he said to me wryly one day. He was no longer goofy Harpo. He was Henry now, or Hank, as some of his buddies called him. He was different and strange. I couldn't reach him. I knew he had been through a bad experience that I knew little about, but he wouldn't talk to me about it ever. I tried to get him to take counseling at college or the Veterans' Hospital, and he did go a couple of times, but lost interest in it. I talked to our family doctor, but Harpo said he had seen doctors make huge mistakes many times and he had lost faith in them too.

He hung around the family's house for the longest time, existing in a kind of paralysis, a state of suspended inaction. We asked all our friends if they had any jobs that Harpo could do. We thought to keep him busy. He took to spending long hours with Nick Iodanza who ran the only gas station in town. Nick was a grizzled, garrulous, quirky man who collected antiques and stored them in his gas station. He was a human squirrel. His station was a small Cape Cod cottage painted bright yellow. I don't even know what brand of gas he sold. I think it was Sunoco. Anyway, two pumps, a little house full of antiques, and Nick holding court all day long and part of the night.

I paid little attention to Nick and his one-man show. I seldom took my car in to him, preferring to tank up on the mainland before taking the ferry over to the island. I usually drove up from New York where I was living now with my wife, Kerry, while trying to launch my acting career. My mother and Harpo were the only family members at home anyway. My father, divorced from my mother, had gone back to Wales, and Jenny was married and living in Connecticut.

Nick was a funny man from what I know of him. He was a Korean war veteran, had never been married, but lived with his mother at the other end of town away from his gas station. Unmarried sons, widowed or divorced mothers, and wars. I wonder if those weren't the elements that initially bonded Harpo to Nick.

Somewhere along the line, Harpo fixed up a garden in Nick's station, a little triangular garden centering around Nick's signs which were hung with hanging baskets of nasturtiums and geraniums; down below, colorful bouquets of impatiens were planted in the ground. Harpo would tend this garden carefully for Nick, watering, weeding, doing whatever needed to be done. And he, along with others in town, where Nick's station was, would spend a lot of time chatting with the affable Nick who had opinions about everything under the sun and was always ready to express them. People would drive in to talk or have a cup of coffee or fill their cars with gas, but often they would go home with some novel little antique Nick had found. When the summer people came at the end of June, they too buzzed around the station, taking a lot of business away from Old Sims' general store, especially after Nick put in a Coke machine and began serving free coffee.

We thought landscaping might be something to interest Harpo, but the only gardens he was at all attentive to were Nick's little one and our mother's extensive ones. Mother finally resorted to calling influential friends. Bob Darnelle, who was a vice-president of a French chemical company, had known us since we were small children. He knew Harpo had studied chemistry in college and spoke French fluently, so he offered him a beginning job in his company in Boston for a year, and then, after that, he assigned Harpo to the Paris office, supposedly for only two years. Harpo must really have shaped up there and done a good job because he lived and worked in Paris for all of ten years.

After Harpo left for France, Nick made a rustic little sign that read "Harpo's Garden" and put it up on a little redwood post in the garden. Then, Nick tended the garden and replenished it with impatiens every year and kept it looking good for the times when Harpo would come home for visits.

Other neighbors replaced Harpo now, stopping by Nick's, not always to buy gas or discuss antiques, but just to chat with Nick and learn what he thought of how the Red Sox were doing, or why did the President do this, or what was his economic forecast. Nick read and thought about a lot of things. Even my mother had only Nick take care of her car now instead of taking it all the way over to Rockland. She claimed Nick and his gas station were the best thing that had ever happened to Spanish Island.

During his years in France, Harpo married and had two sons. I went once to Paris to visit and to see the boys, so I said. Actually, I went because I missed Harpo and wanted to see if he needed my help. He didn't. He was thriving in his new world. His French colleagues and neighbors all responded to the genuine niceness of his disposition. His two little boys were dynamos. I couldn't get over hearing perfect French issue from their cherubic little mouths. Harpo told me his sons had dual citizenship. He said if they chose French citizenship they might automatically have to go into the French army. I think he was afraid of this. He didn't want his or anybody's kids to have to go through what he had.

Mireille, Harpo's wife, was an artist. She painted landscapes, mostly of Provence, and realistic still lifes. She was a very quiet, sweet person. Her temperament reminded me of Harpo himself when he was very young—innocent and optimistic, yet fragile somehow. "Mireille for mirror image," I said to her jokingly once. She didn't know what I meant.

That visit to Harpo in Paris, oddly enough, turned out to be a restorative for me, just as Kerry had hoped it would be. Seeing Harpo making everything work so well somehow reassured me, so that I went back to New York knowing that some uneasiness in my life had finally been settled. Maybe Harpo was just returning a favor.

Back home, I discovered a curious thing happening to me. Whenever I visited my mother, who now was the sole survivor in her household, I drifted over to Nick's place to spend an hour or so. It was almost as though Nick and his station provided some sort of contact for me with Harpo, the grown-up in-between Harpo that I never really knew. Nick displayed letters and postcards he had received from Harpo. There was an inscribed photo of Harpo, Mireille, and their two sons, and Nick bragged about them as though they were his own family. He even told me things about them that I didn't know. Sometimes I felt extremely jealous of the rapport with Harpo that Nick had. Was it my reserved nature or just Nick's magnetism? I envied him the embrace of life he had. Harpo had that same amplitude that included many people in the circle of his warmth. I, with my quiet, introspective ways, felt like some narrow specialist who had missed all the good times. I felt like an outsider.

Some years have passed now. Harpo is gone. He died in his sleep of a massive coronary, brought on by over-work, I always felt. He was not yet forty. Mireille and the children came home with his body. The services were held in the

Spanish Island Congregational Church. Among the mourners, just for the service, not to socialize, Nick sat in the back row, a Catholic come to a Protestant church for his old friend's last rites.

A few days later I stopped by Nick's station to fill up the car with gas. Nick chattered on over-amiably, finally blurting out, "I just can't talk about Harpo now." I saw a man banking down huge emotions. "It's all right," I said. "I understand."

The garden bloomed and was looked after still. When bitter weather wore down the letters that read "Harpo's Garden," they soon were painted bright again. I noticed this through all the seasons, but I never spoke of Harpo to Nick again. However, whenever I drove into his station, an old man would stand up straight again and come alive for a moment as though he thought I was Harpo. And then I would notice a slight slump return to his shoulders when he realized it was only I.

After a while when the rhythms and patterns in my own life settled down again, the news came to me one day in the middle of a rehearsal that Nick was sick and dying of cancer in a hospital in Rockland and then that he was dead. My mother phoned me at a time when I was on the edge of success. But I was determined to go, and so I risked everything and just left. When I arrived at our house, my mother said, "You must come and see." She led me down the road toward Nick's station.

What I saw I could not believe. Overnight, the little gas station had been visited spontaneously by most of the friends and customers that Nick had ever had. There were flowers everywhere. Baskets of them, huge floral tributes, hanging geraniums, store-bought ficus Benjaminas and dracaenas, hand-plucked cottage roses, black-eyed Susans, and daisies, everywhere. Harpo's Garden had burst into glorious bloom.

And news of Nick's passing spread around with the astonishing tale of the nocturnal visitation, so that the news reporters and photographers came over from the mainland,

and the television people came and reported it as a wonder in the modern world that one man should be so remembered by his friends.

And I thought it was too. For a time all the neighbors spruced up their houses and their yards. Smiles seemed to be on everybody's lips. "Hello" and "Good morning" meant something once again. People's steps were a little lighter and they didn't grouse about their troubles so much. They made an effort in honor of what they had lost. The world was a pleasure to behold once more.

I tried to tell all this to the nurse, but she just re-arranged the Renoir bouquet on the window sill in a blurr of impressionism, busy work to distract me from talking. She didn't really want to listen. People in hospitals just want you to go to sleep when you're supposed to. So I gave a little wave and a sort of smile in return to the friendly cloud outside my window. It was the best I could do. It was all I could do.

CHINA

When we were very young, living as we did, on an island off the coast of Maine, the three of us developed an unusual sense of geography. What we read in books did not always match what we saw, experienced, and, most of all, imagined in our daily lives. Oddly, Jenny, Harpo, and I formed a little community of our own, a society that could be quite self-sufficient against adults, the other islanders, summer people, or anything and anybody from the mainland, which, to us, was stranger than Oz or the horrors of Disneyland.

We lived on Spanish Island in "July Blue," our parents' summer house which had been in the family for several generations and had grown to a sizable saltwater farm, although there were no crops there and no animals to speak of, except an occasional resident dog or cat. But Jenny, Harpo, and I farmed starfish, sea urchins, beach glass, quohogs, clams, and rocks of all sorts from the sea mercilessly. We knew the sting of salt spray on our faces and could read the weather well enough without having to spit against the wind. We studied the planets wheeling in the skies at night and, sometimes, could almost touch the meteors blazing through the darkness on August nights, like embers from some now extinguished fire. Because we had so little, we made the most of everything. We turned Sparta into Athens. We didn't need television, we didn't need radios, we didn't need the automobile. We almost didn't need electricity at times.

But we did need one another.

We called our Dad Our-Father-Which-Art-in-Heaven because Harpo began giggling once when we were on one of our forced Sunday expeditions to the island's Congo church. When the minister led us in The Lord's Prayer, Harpo thought he was talking about Dad whom Harpo had seen shaving that morning in the bathroom way up on the third floor of "July Blue" where our mother and father had their bedroom suite. Harpo had climbed up the steep wooden stairs called by us the Stairway to Heaven and had seen our Dad with this great white beard foaming and frothing on his face, making him look "just like God", as Harpo reported it. So naturally that image stuck in his mind and made him laugh out loud in church which, in turn, started a chain reaction in Jenny and me. To the outside world, Dad was a Welshman, a Professor of Geology at Harvard. But we knew him best as an opera singer. Some of his best concerts occurred when he was shaving, as he did each morning with an old-fashioned straight razor that had to be sharpened on a strap first and then applied to the snowfall on his face in a manner as skillful as any surgeon's.

We learned opera via the unearthly sounds floating down from Heaven in the morning. Long before we ever went to an opera house on the mainland, we knew all about Mimi and Rudolpho, Butterfly and Lieutenant Pinkerton, Pappageno and the Queen of the Night, Turridu and Santuzza, Rhadames and Aida. Our Father sang *"Che Gelida Manina"* to Jenny's little white hand. He would delight me with *"Si Puo"* and we would all become clowns, whereupon he would rip off his pretend makeup and costume and sing out *"Vesta La Giubba"* with a wonderful tragic flourish. On festive occasions, he would burst into *"Libiam"* from *La Traviata* and we would all become guests at a great Paris banquet where he would sing *"Un Di Felice"* to our mother. We knew the words, we understood the worlds of these operas because Our Father made them so vivid to us. We also knew about geology, but that was business, that was science, and Our Father always made it clear to us that Art was superior to Science.

Mother, on the other hand, had no artistic abilities to speak of, by her own admission. She had almost flunked art in college once, she told us, but, instead, she was an avid reader and an excellent athlete. She taught us how to swim and dive when we were very young. Our Father couldn't be relied upon because he was a peculiar navigator who would take off his glasses and just strike out in a lashing stroke, swimming straight out to sea, as though heading back to Wales. He didn't think swimming was very important, or much fun, apparently, just something useful for getting from one place to another. Mother, though, could do swan dives and back dives, and had a bronze medal that she had won at some swimming meet she went to when she was seventeen. On special occasions, she would let Jenny wear this medal. It depicted a porpoise-like diver slicing through the air toward the water.

Mother came from Boston on the mainland. She liked the city and said she was a city person. Our Father hated the city and said he could exist only on islands and without crowds around. That was probably why he took to opera so well. You need a large space to do it in, that's certain, with all that mouthing, gesticulating, and horsing around. Mother's mother was Irish and her father was Scottish. Mother said that made her a first-generation immigrant. We always thought that gave her a certain exotic quality, as though she were some kind of a gypsy. We really liked our grandparents. We never knew our father's parents well because his father was a Welsh lawyer who had died young and his mother was an Englishwoman who remarried and went away to South Africa. She wrote our Father once a year at Christmas and always sent him a hand-knitted sweater.

Our Irish grandmother was our favorite. She lived in Boston, if one must describe the place realistically. But, to Jenny, Harpo, and me, she lived in China because that's what we called her house, and we had our reasons. The China that we knew was not the largest country on earth, perhaps the smallest, but it was the richest in ways that many people would never understand. If you drew a map of it, it would have three parts--one red, one blue, and one green. It was populated when we knew it by only about a very few select inhabitants, plus Jenny, Harpo, and me. It was a land of color, contrasts, and imagination. It was the place where the very last and most important commencement of The Marble School was held. It was the land in which Jenny, Harpo, and I were initiated into the adult world. Everything that happened in our lives was different after the partition of China when China was divided and changed, its unity broken forever.

The Marble School was where Jenny, Harpo and I spent most of our time after regular school. The Marble School was a creation of our imaginations and our play, something in which all three of us could participate and gain the approval of our parents. We took the business of education seriously, probably because Our Father was such a good role model for us. Maybe we also just liked being in charge of things or had a taste for order and conformity. I don't know. I don't even remember when it began. Sometime when I was around eight, I'd say, and Jenny ten. I think she dragooned me into it originally. Harpo came into it only toward the end. The Marble School was especially busy on rainy days and after that memorable Christmas when Our Father installed a splendid intercom system from Jenny's bedroom to mine to Harpo's over the garage. It was just what we three wanted for Christmas. It legitimized our childhood efforts at communication and, in our minds at least, elevated us instantly and irrevocably to the rank of professionals. Jenny became Miss Curtis at the age of twelve in charge of the fourth grade. She taught Latin and Spanish as well as English, French, and Math, although she had not yet started studying Spanish herself. She just pieced it together from the Latin and French she knew. I was the homeroom teacher for the third grade and I taught Science, Art, and all sports at the school which, for us, meant sailing, swimming, and ice skating. Harpo was the kindergarten teacher. We let him teach only general stuff because he was so young that he had not yet attended any school. But he did a good job at the Marble School, I'll say that for him.

We lived year round at our family's summer home on Spanish Island. We had lived in Aberystwyth, Wales, and in Cambridge, Massachusetts before this, but somehow we settled in with our parents on this magical island. Later, Our father would leave us and go back to Wales. But at this time, the house seemed warm and snug and we were surrounded by our family's love which insulated us against the cold autumns and winters that roiled up along Maine's coast.

I don't think we ever had or wanted many toys and gadgets in those early days. Jenny, Harpo, and I were self-reliant, the leading virtue of all our island neighbors. One Christmas we received tantalizing boxes of marbles, and we instantly romanticized them, metamorphosing them into exciting individuals, all of whom would become pupils in our little school. We cherished those glassies, agates, and purees and carried them around in the tops of gift boxes from Bloomingdale's, Filene's and Jordan Marsh in which we would swirl them around and watch them spin their dazzling kaleidoscopic dances.

"Miss Curtis," I would call out to Jenny on the phone. "How is John F. Kennedy doing in school?"

"Not as well as he should," she would reply "He needs to do more work in Math. He only managed a C+ on the last exam."

"Thank you," I say. "I will speak to him about it. "Has Sophia Loren gotten off probation yet?"

"Yes," Jenny says. "In fact, she just got an "A" in Geography."

"Good," I reply. Our marbles were not just ordinary students. Many of them were very well-known people. Did you know that Julius Caesar and Joan of Arc both went to our school? Joan was valedictorian when she graduated.

We also produced an outstanding ice skater. Her name was Sonja Henie. She was a blue-green glassie that Jenny discovered in her homeroom. Nobody could spin and turn and shoot out like a jet rocket better than Sonja Henie. I wanted Sonja Henie in my homeroom because we were planning a special ice show one year, so I traded Carl Yastrzemski and President Ford for her. Yaz was a disappointing spinner, "a nice smile, but he lacks grace," as Jenny's homeroom report about him read. President Ford was a bland beige ball who wouldn't move and couldn't jump. Sonja could do everything. She lit up my homeroom the day she arrived.

An interesting experiment is about to occur. Soon we are off to the mainland to visit my grandmother and grandfather in their scary house in China, really Back Bay, Boston. We are taking the whole Marble School on a field trip with us. Harpo didn't want to do this at first. All he thinks of when he is in China is riding the swan boats in the Public Garden, staring at winos in the Common, and getting hotdogs from pushcarts, but Jenny and I persuaded him to bring his marbles along so we can show them to the Empress of China, which is what we call our Irish Grandmother.

However, Jenny and I forgot about that spooky place that is our grandparents' house. It is so old and gloomy that it appears mysterious and frightening to us always. We are afraid of burglars. We are afraid of kidnappers. We are afraid of murderers. This house has been robbed five times. The last time, in the dead of winter, the burglar climbed in through the high window in the pantry. He left huge footprints in the snow. The police were amazed. He must have been some giant of a man.

Once, when burglars broke into the back of the house, my grandmother and my aunt, who was visiting at the time, had to climb out on the roof from my grandparent's bedroom that hangs over the porch down below. Long after midnight, there were my grandmother and aunt, sitting on the roof in their nightgowns, calling for help from the neighbors, wailing like banshees, to hear the Empress tell it. All of this information scares Jenny and me. There is a third floor there, where the three of us kids usually have to sleep. Right across from our room is a dark attic chock-full of all kinds of ancient stuff you could use in a witch's curse, or something. Even worse is the basement, way down below. It is dark and foul-smelling and wanders underneath the entire house. It has a separate entrance from the outside. I am convinced there are four or five burglars and murderers who live in the dark caves down there.

There are some attractions in the house, though. It has stained-glass Tiffany windows, a long polished bannister good for sliding down, a window seat on the lower landing, parlor doors that open and close like a theatre, and a very narrow secret passage of stairs that go up from the kitchen into the servants' quarters. But we don't like the detached garage way out in the back, another hideout for thugs and killers, I am sure.

If you stay away from the evil garage, you can have fun in the garden. We call it The Garden of Eden because my grandfather has an apple tree in the center of it with very few apples on it. But the ones that are there are delicious. I know that for a fact. I plucked an apple from that tree one day and ate it. I didn't realize my grandfather counts the apples. He does. He is Scottish and very fierce. His voice is loud. I was actually trembling when he boomed out, "Who took an apple from my tree?" I was hoping Harpo would get blamed, but he didn't. Harpo is scared of this garden. He is convinced it is the real Garden of Eden. Jenny shot me an angry look when we heard my grandfather's voice, so I knew she wouldn't save the day for me, as she does once in a while. I guess everybody could tell from my shaking and quaking that I was the thief. I was afraid my grandfather would sentence me to permanent hell in the basement along with the other criminals, but he didn't. My grandmother appeared, put her warm arm around my shoulders, and said to my grandfather, "Hush now. You've no business raising your voice like that." Her being Irish accounts for all her good qualities, says my mother.

When Jenny asked Harpo and me who should be our commencement speaker, there was no doubt in my mind that it should be our grandmother. Luckily, Harpo understood completely what a commencement was since he had seen Our-Father-Which-Art-in-Heaven march in those funny academic parades in both Aberystwyth and Cambridge, Mass. Harpo thought the speeches were always boring and he couldn't understand why people laughed and looked around appreciatively to see if others were laughing also. But he liked the picnics under the trees and out of the backs of station wagons and the good mood that the end of commencement always put Dad in. So did we.

"Who do you want as speaker?" Jenny asked Harpo, after she called us all together for our weekly meeting.

"Our Father," said Harpo. "He can wear his monk's outfit, flap his wings, and twirl his tassel."

"Who do you want, Patrick?" Jenny asked me, writing down Harpo's choice on a slip of paper.

"Grandmother," I said. "I love her stories about Ireland. Maybe she will sing."

"Grandmother," wrote Jenny. "Well, Harpo," she said. "I vote for Grandmother, also, so she wins. Sorry."

"That's okay," said Harpo, smiling his little smile, and brushing back his curly mop of hair. "I like Grandmother, too."

"The faculty meeting is over, then," said Jenny. "Please keep this a secret from your pupils. We will tell Grandmother when we get to her house."

"I'm glad it's not Grandpa," said Harpo.

Jenny approaches Mom for more information after our meeting is over. "When are we going to China?" Jenny asks Mom.

"Next week," says Mom. "I want you children to be very quiet while we are there."

"Why?" asks Jenny. "We don't make much noise, do we?"

"No," admits Mom. "You don't, but your grandmother has not been well lately and I don't want you to tire her out."

"We won't," says Jenny, examining Mom's face for further information.

"Grandmother is very ill," Jenny reports to us. "I don't know whether she can do the Commencement speech."

"What's the matter?" I ask.

"Is she going to die?" asks Harpo.

"I hope not," says Jenny.

The one supreme thing about our grandparents' house is the three rooms off the entrance hall. They all have very high ceilings with flowers and vines worked into the white plaster on the ceilings and top mouldings, like those you see in Greek rooms in a museum. But on the floor are three luxurious, beautifully colored Chinese rugs that are a wonderland to the three of us kids. The one in the parlor is blue. There are two great peacocks in the grey field of this one, hanging from the branch of a tree with their long opalescent tails trailing down. The rug in the living room is red. Nightingales sing in a chandelier tree in this one and beautiful blue dragonflies cut through the sky. In the dining room, the rug is green with birds flying around in a golden Chinese heaven. Jenny, Harpo, and I love to lie on these velvety rugs and roll out our marbles, sending them off on exotic adventures. Jenny told us these rugs are accurate artistic depictions of China. She read an article on the emperors of China in *The National Geographic*. This is why we call our grandparents' house China.

The Empress of China sits, not on a jewel-encrusted peacock throne, but on a brown mohair chair with a shawl drawn around her shoulders. She seems old, tired today, but her light blue eyes look deep into the hearts of her grandchildren, as always, and she becomes one with them herself. She is trying to comb her thin, greyish hair. Jenny tries to help by taking the comb from Grandmother's hand. Jenny tries to fluff up that thin silver silk. She wants to make her beautiful. She cannot. The Empress smiles at Jenny, as though she understands. She is gentle, a friend. Our mother comes in to pull us away from her. The Empress reaches out her fingers to mine. We touch in parting, fingertips to fingertips, as though one of us is drowning. Harpo looks at me to see my reaction. He is learning.

I think about what I know, what good times we have lived through. I know her name is Mary Flood and that she comes from Castlemartyr in County Cork. I know she had long auburn hair when she was seventeen and that she became a nurse and was much admired on the boat to America because of her beautiful hair. My mother has that same color hair and mine is that color, also. Jenny has dark wavy hair and Harpo has a mop of blond curly hair that looks like Harpo's wig, which is why he was named after the great comedian. Mary Flood met my grandfather when he was a patient in St. James Hospital in New York City. He was a tough Scotsman named Angus MacVuirach but, as he told us, he knew Mary Flood was a fine broth of a woman, the only one destined to become the love of his life. So he married her, and they went to Boston to live where he worked in the export trade. Mary loved Boston. "Glory be," she would tell people. "It's got a whole Irish section. St. Paddy's Day here is more important than it is in Dublin."

The Empress loved to show us the sights and sounds of Boston. We would walk down Beacon Street and she would point out the purple glass in the bow windows of the finest houses. We would all skip together sometimes through the Common and marvel at the flowers in the Public Garden in the Spring. Harpo would always ride with Grandmother in the swan boat. Our Father once stood on the shore singing "O Evening Star" from *Tannheuser*, embarrassing all of us who were on the boat because somebody said "Look at that kook, will you?" We all pretended not to know him and then dissolved in laughter when he tried to join us back on shore.

We always had good times with the Empress. She would tell us about the horses of Ireland, and the suds, and the leprechauns and wee folk.

"Tell us about home," Jenny would beg. She loved to hear about Grandmother's hometown.

"Home was quite simple," Grandmother would say. "Me father was the stone mason in town, so of course the Floods have the grandest tombstones you've ever seen in the bone orchard there. We had a thatched roof and an earthen floor, very typical of the houses in Castlemartyr, which is quite poor, like all the towns in Ireland. At the far end of town, was the big castle of the rich lord, who was sent from England long ago to snoot it over all of us Irish with that arrogant superiority only the English have got."

"Is Ireland green the way it looks on our globe?" asked Harpo.

"Oh, it's green all right," she replied. "But different from your own Spanish Island with its rocks and dark pines. You see, there are all those winds and mists that chase around Ireland all the time, giving it a softness, a beginning-of-spring-like look. It's a lovely, fair place, I think. Some parts of Martha's Vineyard remind me of it, especially Chilmark, I'd say.

"Tell about the play," I say. "Cathleen, the Hooligan."
Jenny and Harpo laugh.

"No, no, darlin'," she says. "*Cathleen ni Houlihan.* Don't
be blaspheming her good name, will you? It was written by a
poet named Willie Yeats. It's the story of an old, wrinkled
woman, very worn and ancient, who becomes a beautiful
young woman again through the force of magic and
imagination."

I love to hear my grandmother tell about this play. It's
like a song, to hear her tell it, with her voice rising and falling
in the lilting music of it. An idea strikes me. "Tell the truth,
Grandmother. Wasn't that play really written about you?"

Jenny and Harpo watch her reaction. They have the same
thought too.

"No, no, darlin'" she says, bending down to kiss my
forehead. "Not just about me. About *all* Ireland."

It's over and done with now, "ancient history," as the
Empress might put it . The Commencement was held in the
living room on the red rug. The valedictorian, polished with
Windex, sat in the middle on the tail of one of the
nightingales. The salutatorian was placed on the other. The
audience was composed of Grandmother, sitting in her
mohair chair, Our Father and Mother. Grandpa, fortunately,
was out of town. We didn't need any Scottish skeptics there.

Jenny, Harpo, and I moved our classes of marbles up to
their locations. The whole place looked to me like a great
cathedral of learning. My class was stationed just below one of
the great blue dragonflies with the best students stretched out
on the wings. Harpo's class was down near the bottom of
the rug around the base of the great branched tree because
they were just Beginners.

Grandmother gave the address. She said how pleased she
was to be invited to this august ceremony. (This made Harpo
laugh because he thought Grandmother had made a mistake.
"It's June, not August," Harpo explained. But Jenny cut him

off with a withering glance. She hates anybody who has "a deficient vocabulary," as she puts it. But Grandmother pressed on, saying that our pupils looked to be a good lot and that she thought they would be destined for great things if only they gave their imaginations wings. She spoke about soaring and dreaming and of the pursuit of perfection that is somewhere far above us. (I was so pleased she said that because, luckily, there was my entire class sitting on or near the very wings of the most perfect dragonflies in all China.) When she asked who the valedictorian was, I spoke up proudly and told her it was Sonja Henie. Then Sonja did her spinning act in a box top from a Lord and Taylor's box left over from Jenny's birthday. Grandmother applauded and so did Our Father and Mother. Then the salutatorian was introduced. He was in Jenny's class. His name was Winslow Homer and Jenny said he had painted many pictures of the Maine coast, including Spanish Island. I was not too pleased because Winslow Homer was not good at sports and he was late to my class too many times, but Jenny had seen an exhibit of his paintings in Portland and nothing could stop her once she made up her mind about something.

When the program was finished, all those who graduated went into one corner of China and all the others were moved into their new places. Ten pupils got left back. I flunked Marilyn Monroe and Elvis Presley. Jenny flunked Plato, Victoria Regina, and Ludwig von Beethoven. Harpo flunked all the rest. They were friends of his, not really important people, so that doesn't matter so much. It will take him a while to catch on. At the very end Our Father was going to sing "Land of Hope and Glory," but Grandmother felt faint and so he and Mother helped her to her room. We all had tollhouse cookies courtesy of Grandmother who had put them out on the big library table for us.

We saw the Empress of China only once more after that. She was propped up in an ocean of pillows in her huge mahogany bed and could barely smile and wave at Jenny, Harpo, and me. She was dying of cancer, Jenny whispered to me before we went in to her house, and Harpo overheard. We brought flowers to her. I presented them to her. Her fingers seemed to want to touch mine rather than hold the flowers. The nurse said we could stay only five minutes, but Harpo spoiled it all by beginning to cry, and so the nurse pushed us out of the room. We had only that one last minute with her. I just had time to present her with a card I had made. It showed an emerald green nightingale flying through the night. Underneath, I had written in green ink "Imagination has wings."

When she was gone, a great heaviness came down on all of us. Our Father didn't sing while shaving in the mornings and Mother had to make many hurried trips to Boston. The news was that our grandfather was not taking it well. Within a year, he was gone also. "Dead of a broken heart," said our Mother. "He just couldn't survive without her. Some people are like that." Jenny took me aside then and told me, but not Harpo, because she didn't think he'd understand, that our grandparents were actually exactly like Romeo and Juliet, star-crossed lovers who couldn't live without each other.

The last trace of this period in our lives was when they broke up the house in Boston. Everything went to different places. The piano went to a friend, clothing went to the Goodwill and the Society of St. Vincent de Paul, some paintings were sold, the Chinese rugs were rolled up to go into storage, and finally the house itself was sold to a man who planned to make apartments in it for Emerson, Harvard, and B.U. students. Harpo watched the moving men take the rugs out to the van. "China is gone forever," he said.

Over the months, life sorted itself out and continued, bringing new interests to all of us. Our Father gradually went back to singing, Harpo finally learned to conquer his fear of water and learned how to swim, I began making a collection of waterbugs, and Jenny developed a sudden interest in Simon Carruthers, the new delivery boy in the General Store. Mother sifted through cartons brought up from Boston, saving some things, throwing other things out. From time to time she would show us her treasures. One day she found a card in the shape of a shamrock, colored in green crayon, reading "Miss Curtis' Fourth Grade wishes you 'Top of the Morning,'" another day a note written in my shakiest, most scared handwriting, reading,

> Dear Grandfather,
>   I am sorry I stole one apple.
>   Like,
>   Patrick

I wonder if he realized I was withholding love?

Also discovered were some secret poems, expressing loneliness and sadness, written at times when my grandfather was away on business. These were in my grandmother's handwriting. None of us knew she wrote, but all of us knew she felt and cared.

Over the years, the rugs that were once China came out of storage and went to different places, but they were never united under one roof again. The blue one went with Harpo to Paris when he married Mireille, the green one went with Jenny to Connecticut along with the big library table from our grandparents' living room, and the red one went with me to California to be the centerpiece in a panelled family room in a world where nobody plays marbles anymore, where only mutants play mindless games of war and destruction.

STARFISH

I knew it happened all the time, but what I didn't realize is why it happened. That's not so surprising if I'm honest with myself. Actually, I'm a real Dumbo in the sky, not the great Jellico Lamos all my friends know and love. My reputation for being a giant brain is just somebody else's opinion of me, not mine. I mean, how many times do you have to be the last person chosen up for the team, even if they do use a baseball bat and hands on and all that, making it look like some democratic process, which it isn't? God, you have to be really stupid not to be able to figure it out. You'd think I'd get wise when I saw that it was always happening to Homer, Piggy Balls, and me. Why were we always lumped together as though we were some dumb bunch of three musketeers or something?

"Homer, will you get out of my way, please? I can't walk home with you today."

"Why not?"

"I'm meeting Brian.",

"Big deal. How come?"

"None of your business."

"You going to the Dry Res?"

"No. Math."

"Oh."

"See you later."

"I'll whistle. After dinner."

"Sure."

Toujours, after dinner, Homer comes by and whistles. It irritates my foster mother, Mrs. Hamilton. She says some of the paying guests in our boarding house think it's funny. It disgusts my sister, Esdra. She gets up and leaves the table. She can't stand Homer. None of the girls can. And you know why? It embarrasses me even to think about it. There he is whistling for me to come out after dinner just so we can go through the forest under cover of night to hide behind a spreading pine tree and stare up at Gloria Calabrese's lighted window. Does Homer think Gloria is totally stupid, or what? He's always waiting for a look, usually around nine o'clock. He thinks Gloria knows he's looking and he thinks she wants him to see something. That's what he always says. Piggy Balls and I have to wait with him, and we have never seen anything yet. God, it's boring waiting with this fool who has his pockets and his wallet full of Trojans which we know he'll never get to use.

Homer is blond and white-faced and has this whacked-off John F. Kennedy half-dollar-sized gland he's always showing off. Sex is all he ever thinks of and talks about. Piggy, though, is okay, kind of pink and bouncy, as though he's made of rubber. He's not too bright, but he has a nice disposition and he has never said a mean word about anyone, including Homer and me, and so that makes him a good friend. I feel I can really trust him.

I don't know how I ever got elected into this little trio. Caesar, Pompey, and Antony, my sister calls us. I have no idea who might be who. All I know is that I am my usual self—black-haired, skinny beyond belief, and so ashamed of my bony body and all this strange sexual bulging that's happening that sometimes I am truly sorry I am a human being at all. I mean, I don't need a high-powered set of binoculars to see that none of the girls we know is remotely interested in Homer, Piggy, or me. Don't we have any sex appeal at all? Are we all homos and don't know it? Am I going to have to become a priest or a eunuch, or something? I worry about these things at night. Sometimes I am sorry that I have this giant brain that makes me read Shaw and Shakespeare and D. H. Lawrence ahead of my time and actually like them. Why couldn't I have turned out like the other kids with a slew of comic books and tacky soap operas to come home to?

Actually, books are not the really big thing in my life right now. Baseball is. I'd really like to hit a baseball occasionally—just a modest hit, a nice single or double, to prove to Brian,

Jeff, and Jimbo that I am worth paying attention to. But it never happens. I'm always the last or the next-to-last chosen for the team, and then there I am, standing like a damn fool way out in left field, watching a fly ball sail in, which appears to be like two balls, one of which is the right one, which invariably hits me right in the face and makes the whole team laugh. Try and brush that stuff off when you repeat it two or three times a week. Wimpishness is just in my nature, I guess. I notice that Brian eats two hamburgers, an order of large fries, and a chocolate frappe after every game. Me, I split an order of fried clams and onion rings with Piggy, and order a small tonic. My plate looks like a Japanese flower arrangement when you stop to think about it.

"Jellico, come in now. Dinner is ready."
"Yo-ho." That's my standard macho reply to my mother. Who am I fooling?
Baseball. I think about it all through dinner. Father Jim, who coaches the C.Y.O. team, thinks it is an important test of character. He's convinced me of this. He said he thinks I am not trying hard enough. He says I obviously can run fast and should be able to steal bases and all. He said he thinks Piggy would be better in wrestling. I think he's right. Piggy is hard to catch and can really push when he doesn't bounce around. Father Jim says Homer should lay off beating the bishop so much. Says nothing good will happen to Homer until he does. Homer ignores him, of course.
The baseball field we usually play on adjoins the Dry Reservoir, a wonderful desert of blank spaces and red conduits you can crawl through and down into an excavation that looks like a bombed-out brick building. The Dry Res provided water for our little island for years until it was replaced with a whole new system. The Dry Res was the Sahara to us. We played Lawrence of Arabia there and rode imaginary camels over the sand dunes to the beach at Point Diablo where we discarded the towels from our sweating heads and jumped naked into the briny deep on Bareass

Beach into water that generally was 55 to 60 degrees. Homer of course, always made a big splash and a great hoopla of noise, but I notice he was the first one out, shivering on the beach, looking for driftwood to build a fire. What a coward!

Another odd thing about Homer: Once he found a starfish on the sand, pulled it apart in three pieces and gave two of them to Piggy and me. "Now, throw them out to sea," he said. "We have each made a new starfish out of one."

I'm embarrassed. I am watching something sexy on the tv. My mother just walked into the room. Homer was right behind her. I quickly flicked off the remote, but I think I was too late. They both saw. I just know it. That creep. Why didn't he whistle this time?

My mother leaves us alone. She is so polite. She's English. Little does she know that Homer is a sex fiend.

"Hi, Homer. What's going down?" The minute I said it I knew it was typically stupid. Dumbo in the sky!

There is a rush of urgency in Homer's voice. "Brian is over at Sheila's house."

"You're kidding!"

"Let's go. Piggy, Jimbo, Jeff, and Don are over there too. Gloria and Didi said they might come by."

Through the hot night to Sheila's house in the Cobb's Point area. Tree toads singing in the elms and pines. Street lamps throwing down focused pools of light. My God, they're in the back seat of Sheila's mother's Mercedes.

"Where's Mrs. McLaren?"

"She's playing bridge. Shut up, Piggy. You'll spoil everything." Homer in charge now, organizing his musketeers.

In the car, shadows cutting through the light.

"Holy Toledo," says Homer.

"Maximum," says Piggy.

"Homer," I say. "Is this your idea of a good time?"

"Shut up, you sphincter," says Homer.

I shut up. I look into the car. Nothing I see is remotely human. All I see is an abstract pattern probably made by the branches of the low-hanging tree dripping pine cones over the driveway and car. If Brian and Sheila are actually in there, they are well down below the water line.

Jeff and Jimbo cruise up along the sidewalk. I see they have Susan and Penny with them.

"Take a hike, Homer," Jimbo says, shoving Homer aside.

"Come on, guys. Let's go," Homer says to Piggy and me, as though we had other plans anyway. We retreat, walking half a block away. Homer picks up a stone and tries to knock out a street light. He fails. "Oh, hell," he says. "They couldn't get Gloria to come out. Did you notice that?"

I am at the optometrist's over in Rockland having my eyes examined. "How old are you?" asks the doctor.

"Thirteen."

"And you've never worn glasses?"

"The school nurse said my eyes were okay."

"You have astigmatism. You see double. Look at this light. How many points of light do you see?"

"Two."

"We'll correct that. Now, look at these bars, those that are vertical and those that are horizontal."

"Kids of America, eye glasses changed my life. Run right now to your local eye doctor for a new lease on life." That's my crazy idea for a television commercial. But it's true. I'm a Clark Kent in reverse. It doesn't matter that Homer and even Piggy laughed at me when they first saw my glasses. "Four-eyed monster with the Tolstoy tilt," they labeled me because I was lugging *War and Peace* around with me after school. Their laughter soon stopped when baseball season came around again. Guess who began seeing, and catching, and running, and pitching? Guess who began to be Numero Uno chosen for any baseball team you could name that we played on? Zowie!

"Hey, Jellybean, not bad. I want you to pitch for our team." Can you believe that Brian actually said those very words to me? That really changed my life. It was so long, Piggy and Homer, and hello, Sheila and Brian and Jimbo and Penny. And guess who wound up with Gloria Calabrese in the back seat of a Dodge Dart one night? Don't worry. We talked about *Hamlet*, which we both had seen and I had read, and Gloria said she identified so much with Ophelia that she thought she should read the play too. I liked this, but was a little confused, because if she was Ophelia, was I Hamlet, or Laertes, and what did all that mean? Anyway, it sure made Homer jealous. It served him right for misjudging Gloria so completely. What does he know?

I am a senior now in high school. I have my sights set on college in the fall. I am captain of the baseball team, editor of the school newspaper, a member of the National Honor Society, and winner of the four-year Geoffrey Siebold Cobb Scholarship for Academic Excellence, following in my sister's footsteps. I tell people I want to be a sportswriter or announcer, but I am not really certain about that. I say it because my mother says it sounds like a sensible thing to do, and everybody appears to like a definite answer. It reassures them somehow, I can tell. I think it may be time for me to leave this island and these friends. I haven't really traveled much. I know only a few things—something about boats, tides, books, and baseball—very little about women, technology, and city subways. I suppose it's time I learned. Our guidance counselor told me I should apply to Columbia University. She said they have a good school of journalism there, but somebody told me Columbia is in a very tricky neighborhood.

When I put my glasses on, I can see clearly now. The world no longer is an undecipherable blur. I don't see Homer or Piggy much. They drifted away from me somehow, as if that should surprise anybody. I notice that they have taken up with a new student from Sweden named

Ollie. Somebody told me he has leukemia and that his days are numbered. He's a tall stringbean who always wears grey corduroy pants. What an odd combination the three of them make—Ollie, the dying Swede, Piggy, the bouncing ball, and Homer, the eighty-year old kid. I catch them out of the corner of my eye. Sometimes I even feel a little sad about them, a little sorry about something. But I don't know about what. Once I saw the three of them walking along the beach and I almost joined them. But I didn't. A starfish washed up by my feet and surprised me. I kicked it back into the sea. It didn't matter anyway.

When I got home that day my mother handed me a letter that had arrived in the mail. She said it contained good news, that I was accepted to Columbia for the fall term. I thought that'll show them all. Esdra said it was a tremendous opportunity for me to go to New York and get all that education. She said New York was almost as good as Boston where she had gone. I thought so too. But now I'm not so sure. I wish I hadn't booted that dumb starfish. What harm did it ever do to anyone?

THE EYE OF THE PIANO

I began composing music and giving concerts when I was eight years old. I had been storing it up for years. One Saturday night in August when my parents had invited six couples thought to be the artistic community of our small island off the coast of Maine, I appeared dramatically during cocktails at the door to the living room that gives out to the terrace and the sea beyond and just lurked lazily against the evening sky until old lady McLarty said, "Oh, there's Patrick," and smiled her red crocodile smile at me.

"How's that big boy doing today?" boomed out Judge Herrick Williams, my boy scout leader. I paused and smiled tentatively in that shy way I'd seen my younger brother, Harpo, do many times and get away with it because people thought it was cute, and then I heard my father answer, "Just fine. Did you know he's playing the piano now?"

"No, I didn't," said the judge.

"Well, Patrick, isn't that something?" said Mrs. McLarty, swirling the ice cubes in her glass for a refill.

That was my cue. My father nodded to me, saying, "Oh, yes. Play something Patrick."

I remember I bowed and announced that I would be playing Opus 1, No. 3. There was a curious silence and an ominous clinking of glasses as guests set down their martinis to see what on earth the older Curtis boy had come up with this time. I slid into home base at the Steinway with what I thought was a professional flourish, swiped from Victor Borge, whom I had seen on television. You sit down smartly, brush off imaginary tails, then turn and stare the audience straight in the eyes just daring them to laugh at you. Then you turn, lower your head, hunker up your shoulders and play something inner and personal as though you're thinking through the piano. I was determined to knock the olives right out of that audience's drinks.

I launched into a wildly atonal nightmare that Schoenberg would have flinched at, but which might have spoken to Philip Glass or Villa-Lobos groupies. I played largely with stiff, splayed fingers and lots of fist, but nobody could say I played tepidly. I remember after my soft, hypnotic opening when I began getting into it, Mrs. McLarty noisily picked up her glass and drained her martini. I could hear the sucking noise she made as she wheezed it down her throat, and then a huge, high-pitched nervous laugh came out of her, hovering over the room like a rude counterpoint to my masterpiece.

I thundered now in desperation, arpeggios up, rolling fists down, roaring to a cataclysmic conclusion in which I leaped up, straddled the piano and plucked a string in Franz Lizst's manner until it vibrated throughout the room sealing the doom of the wicked witch's hysterical giggle. When it was over there was a significant silence. I heard Mrs. Jessup, from the Spanish Island Congregational Church, say, "My, that certainly shows expression, or feeling, or whatever it is that's inside you."

"Yes, doesn't it?" my mother said in a weak voice. What a coward my mother was.

"That calls for applause," said my great father, leading the guests in a forced round of applause that grew stronger as the guests finally realized they were witnessing the birth of a new talent. I smiled, thinking how brilliant I was to be revealing my very soul to them, and bowed arrogantly like a demented stage brat. I immediately ran upstairs to find Harpo and Jenny to tell them how triumphant I was in yet another appearance before our family's guests. Jenny had only her scholarship to dazzle people with, Harpo had only his comic looks and sappy smile, but I had a gift. Everybody agreed to that.

Perhaps to put an end to my overly self-indulgent banging at the piano, which is what Harpo and Jenny scornfully called it, Mother arranged for me to take piano lessons from Mrs. Loring, who was offering to teach piano for the first time. Mrs. Loring, I gathered, was someone Mother knew from the Spanish Island Congo Church Ladies' Aid Society. Mother set up an appointment for me to go with her on a Saturday morning at 9:00 a.m. on a sunny day in May, just before my ninth birthday. This was to be my parent's birthday present to me, and I was to play some of my own compositions for this woman who knew a great deal about music, my mother said, and came from Vermont where she had studied at the University of Vermont and then at the Juilliard School in New York. Mother warned me that learning to play properly would involve *labor omnia vincit* and discipline which she, frankly, doubted I had. I assured her I had them all right, and Dad reinforced this by assuring Mother, "Patrick works hard and gets things accomplished, no question about that." With such support behind me, there was no way I was going to let him down. By this time, anyway, I had explored the whole structure of our parlor grand and had taken to lifting up the lid of the Steinway and making strumming sounds, like a sprung zither, in the middle of some of my compositions. Mother, Harpo, and Jenny all said this was bad for the piano, but Dad staunchly reminded them that where art was concerned the piano was a mere wooden instrument. He never said it, but I later thought maybe he believed he had a little Amadeus in me. At any rate, my goal in life then was to please, not to disappoint.

Mother and I walked over to Mrs. Loring's house. As soon as I saw it, I was amazed. I had noticed this strange residence before and wondered about it, but I never knew a piano teacher lived there. You must remember that on our island off the coast of Maine most of the houses are plain Cape Cod cottages, maybe three or four farms with barns, a row of sea captains' houses with fancy widows' walks on top and all of them weatherbeaten and greying like people in a retirement home. But Mrs. Loring actually lived in a real Spanish hacienda—a salmon-colored stucco structure with a red-tiled roof, looking as though it had been blown there by an imaginative storm from Florida, California, or the south of France. She lived in a villa. I couldn't believe it. Piano lessons would certainly take on a new meaning for me if I could regularly visit this exotic palace.

"So this is Patrick," a well-modulated, educated voice issued from a tall, thin woman who peered down at me with vast amusement dancing in her brown eyes. "You've been giving concerts and performing your own compositions, I hear. Is that right?."

"Yes," I said warily. Something told me right off the bat that she had it in for me.

"Play something," she said casually, waving her hand toward the piano.

I stopped, hesitated, because there were two pianos—a rinky-dink upright of the kind usually found in old houses in Maine, and another, a baby grand, filling up most of an interior room behind this one, in which, I could also see a man sitting in a chair reading music scores with a floor lamp casting a golden light down on him and his reading, as though he were in a theatre. I started to sidestep the old upright and headed for the baby grand in the more intriguing other room. "No, not that one," said Mrs. Loring. "This one." She indicated the upright and lifted the cover, watching to see what I would do next.

I was scared.

"Go ahead," she said, pointing to the piano bench. "Move it back."

I did so and sat down.

She motioned my mother to a chair and then she stationed herself rigidly behind me, like some sinister New England coatrack. "Play," she commanded.

I was paralyzed. "I can't," I said.

"Go ahead, Patrick," said my mother with a tremor in her voice.

"If you've been giving concerts and performances," said Mrs. Loring, her voice rippling up and down with superior amusement as she said it, "you have nothing to fear. I have heard you're an old pro. Mrs. McLarty told me you're on to something. Go ahead. Begin."

Trapped. The old croc must have given me a strange review. I thought of Dad, of his confidence in me. I pulled out the bench, sat down, drew it in closer, looked at Mrs. Loring as the piano bench made an unwelcome scraping sound--it didn't seem to faze her--and so I began to play something. It sounded awful because I was shaky and uncomfortable at first, but, then, I thought, that skinny witch isn't going to boss me around, I'll show her, so I began taking off, sliding down so that my right foot hit the sostenuto pedal which made an embarrassing thumping sound. I soared for maybe two minutes on my burst of self-confidence; then I quit in mid-flight and dropped my hands down to my side. I looked at her. "I couldn't reach that pedal too well," I said in a strangulated, quiet voice.

"I noticed that," she said. "A bad pianist sometimes equates loudness with quality. You want to watch out for that."

"I will," I said. Had I passed or flunked?

"I don't know what to say," said Mrs. Loring, addressing my mother. "I don't teach the Maté system. I'm strictly Czerny-Lizst-Leschetizsky, which approaches it from the point of view of technique, not interpretation. Patrick is putting the cart before the horse, if you ask me. He has a feeling, a touch, but there is absolutely nothing behind it. Nothing at all."

She said this with such Yankee emphasis that I felt like some dumb clod-hopper who had stumbled into her lair. I wished that my mother and I could clear out of there. I decided I didn't want piano lessons after all, not even in this dark museum of books, pianos, and a mystery man poring over secret music manuscripts in his red velvet plush chair.

"I think that's what he wants." I heard my mother say. "Technique. Isn't that what you want, Patrick?"

"Yes," I said unconvincingly. I couldn't look at her or Mrs. Loring and tell a lie like that. I focused on the light in the other room and the island of shiny black baby grand.

"Let's see if we can work out some kind of schedule then," said Mrs. Loring. Done. My goose was cooked now. She would barbecue me, I could see that. Happy birthday, Patrick. God, what a lousy birthday it would be.

Eleanor Loring was probably the most influential teacher in my early years, apart from my parents. I learned the usual *World Almanac* stuff about her—she had been born and raised in Steeplechurch, Vermont. Her mother had been a piano teacher and her father a farmer (raised corn and had a stand out on the road), she had a sister named Eugenia who had died and left a son, Hartley, about my age who would be coming to visit the Lorings in June. He lived with the grandparents in Vermont instead of with his father, whom nobody liked, for some reason. She, Eleanor Hartley Loring, had married Chandler Loring, who was somewhat older than she was, when she was a music student at Juilliard and he was singing in the church choir at Marble Collegiate Church in New York which she used to go to on Sundays. He had had some horrendous experience in World War II—been shot down, imprisoned, escaped, recaptured—something so terrible that he couldn't or wouldn't talk about it ever. It had made him anti-social. Only Mrs. Loring could work with him. He was an agronomist, did hybrid experiments in their backyard, but preferred dahlias as a hobby. He also sang tenor at our Congo Church and Mother had deemed his voice "magnificent" when she heard him sing Handel's *Messiah*. He and Mrs. Loring had had one son, Dennis, a tall, gangly individual who loathed music and was interested only in baseball and racing cars. He was currently working in a motorcycle shop in Laconia, New Hampshire. Eleanor Loring preferred not to talk about Dennis or to divulge much information about Mr. Loring. She preferred to talk about Hartley who apparently was a musical prodigy who was being taken under the wing of the Curtis Institute of Music in Philadelphia; all very hush-hush, Mrs. Loring confided. "He's being groomed." I was very impressed and could hardly wait until June to see a person my age who had been selected by those in the know because of his talent.

Other things I learned about Mrs. Loring: She took colonic irrigation regularly, whatever that was. I had the impression it meant enemas, and, indeed, before my piano lessons began, she would come into the room smelling very antiseptic, like getting a whiff from a suddenly-opened medicine cabinet. She also believed in osteopaths, who manipulated her bones, apparently, when she went over to the mainland on her monthly trips to Portland. She was strong on duties and responsibilities, getting to places on time and finishing on time—all those things my other Spanish Island teachers preached at us. She rewarded good work and effort by pasting stickers of butterflies, birds, or stars on your music as you went. She wrote comments with a #2 pencil and changed the rests and notes whenever she felt there had been a typo.

During an actual lesson, Mrs. Loring was very helpful and friendly. Performing the music properly was obviously her chief aim with me. But the whole first week was excruciatingly impossible because we did not sit down at the piano at all, but, instead, sat at her dining room table with a paper chart of piano keys under my hands. The arch of the hand was very important to her. To help me, she placed a ping pong ball in the palm of each hand. I had to arch my hands and hold on to these balls. Then, the fingers had to be regarded as hammers, each one lifting independently as high and as slowly as possible; lift and release. Now, strike. This wasn't easy.

But the worst problem for me was the wrists. Mrs. Loring insisted these had to be relaxed and kept down. Under no circumstances, could you raise your wrists. That indicated tension and playing from the shoulders which she would not tolerate. At home, I had to drum on our dining room table for the first week to strengthen my hands. Harpo came around to look. It annoyed me, the way he was bugging me. I could see that involuntary smile creeping in. So I began tapping out messages to him as though I were banging on some tribal drum. Harpo got the message. "Mom," he shouted out, "Patrick's drumming out 'Harpo is a dummy.'"

"No, I'm not," I said.

"Yes, you are. Listen to him, Mom."

"I'm tapping out 'Harpo is a shit head,'" I said.

Harpo burst into tears and went running off to tell Jenny.

"Don't tease him," Mom said to me.

"He's such a baby," I said. "He knows nothing about art."

It turned out that my hands were not sufficiently strengthened in a week. Mrs. Loring prescribed two more weeks of this for at least an hour a day. I followed her advice faithfully, even performing my finger exercises during boring times in school. Then, at the end of the third week, she finally brought me to the piano--the wretched upright. I soon learned that this was where I would be billeted in her house. Only after about two years and considerable progress in my skills would I be permitted to touch her sacred Baldwin baby grand, which was smaller than our Steinway at home, if you can believe it. But she taught me the difference between a Baldwin and a Steinway and told me that most good American pianists were divided into two camps, Steinway people and Baldwin people. Apparently, the Steinway had a rich, sonorous tone, but a looser action, and action was all-important to Mrs. Loring. The Baldwin was known for its tight action, which meant the fingers didn't have to push the keys down so far, so that a pianist could control his or her touch better. She also told me the whole Steinway Company had had a very checkered career, beginning well, going through some bad times when inferior Steinways were made, and now on a rise again, but maybe it was too late because now you could buy a Japanese Yamaha which had some of the qualities of the Steinway at half the price.

Such information was fascinating to me, particularly since so expert an adult teacher as Eleanor Loring was confiding this news to me, a mere pupil, for I had now accepted my role as novice and was hungry to learn.

The drop-roll was vital to correct technique. That was another of Mrs. Loring's emphases. You had to drop-roll properly.. This meant lifting up the whole arm from the keys with the hand trailing after, rolling it up in the air and then dropping it down on the keys in place so that all the finger-hammers could begin their pecking number again. At first I balked, because it looked so lady-like that I was afraid my friends would think I was effeminate if they caught me doing it. I never let Harpo see me drop-roll at the piano, I can tell you, not until years later after he had studied piano with Mrs. Loring himself and knew how important it was.

Posture, too, had to be paid attention to. One had to sit straight, placing "one's buttocks"— Mrs. Loring's words— "squarely on the bench underneath you, feet pointing toward the floor." Fortunately, I was growing during the years I studied with her so that eventually my feet touched the floor where the magical three pedals lay that held endless fascination for me, especially the one on the far right, the sostenuto, which gave me that sustained, ringing, soaring, inter-galactic sound I loved so well.

But another precept was an even harder cross for me to bear in my early training as a piano student. Mrs. Loring would brook no composing and no performing in public by me. I had to swear to this on my word of honor. "You do not play in public until you are ready," she said. "You will not be ready until I say so." God, as though I were some half-baked muffin you shoved into the oven until it came out golden brown. To impress how important this dictum was, Mrs. Loring told me about Hartley who did not perform in public at all, even though everyone agreed that he was a musical phenomenon with the bridge of his hand being unusually broad and his fingers able to span an octave and a half. And he only ten years old, a tad older than I.

One other thing: Before each lesson, Mrs. Loring carefully placed a rubber mat under the pedals and under both sets of our feet beneath the piano. She was afraid of the violent thunderstorms that swept over the island in the summer. Of course, a lesson could not be terminated because of this irrational human fear of meteorology, but, just in case lightning ever should strike, we would be prepared and, presumably, would just drop-roll it off our wrists and nimble fingers onto the floor somewhere. Mrs. Loring was a devout Congo church advocate. She told me that all the people who went to that church were special people, elected by God to receive his eternal blessing when that time should come, but she also said she believed that if you were going to go, you were going to go. "If our time is up, Patrick," she said to me. "Our time will be up, but, in the meanwhile, let's be sure we keep that rubber mat planted firmly underneath our feet."

I kept my promise. I stifled my mad desire to improvise and compose. I hid my golden light from the island world. I no longer played for guests or talked about my work. I just practiced and suffered and waited.

In June, as promised, Mrs. Loring's nephew, Hartley, the genius from Philadelphia, arrived with Grandmother Hartley for a month's visit. I could hardly wait to meet him. Happily, there he was at my Saturday morning lesson. Mrs. Loring said he would be my first audience and critic and that I was to play some exercises from my Hanon and "Silent Snow, Secret Snow" from *Keyboard Attacks*. He was taller than I, straight dark hair, bright olive eyes, looking like Pinocchio, I thought. But he sat there, chin resting in the palm of one hand, like some ancient sage. "Very good," he said, when I finished. "You played that very well. Let me see your hand." I held out my hand to him. He turned it over and examined it. "Good," he said. "You have short fingers. That's better for a pianist.

You don't want those long, thin, tapering fingers. You need a percussive effect. Who is your favorite composer?"

"Chopin," I said. "I'm going to learn his 'Etude in E-flat' soon."

"Very lyrical and romantic," said Hartley. "Mine's Mozart, and, of course Rachmaninoff, because the parallels are there."

"He doesn't know what you're talking about," said Mrs. Loring.

"Hartley," shouted his unseen grandmother from the dining room. "Are you talking too much again?"

"Be quiet, Grandma," said Hartley. "Do you know anything about Rachmaninoff's life?" he asked me.

"Not really," I said.

"Do you want to hear me play?" he asked.

"Yes," I said.

He got up, sat down at the piano, lifted his hands high in the air and said, "Mozart as played by Fats Waller." Then out came a barrel-house version of the "Rondo alla Turca." Next he imitated Chopin playing "Chattanooga Choo Choo," then Gershwin playing Bach, Dave Brubeck playing "The Habanera" from *Carmen*. For almost an hour, a cascade of melodies and inventions issued from the old upright, until his parrot of a grandmother ended it all with a "Hartley, no more thumping away to show off. That's final." Groaning a sheepish, "Yes, Grandma," he closed the lid as though to fend off further temptation, and said to me, "Let's go over to your house."

That summer, Hartley made many stellar appearances in our home. He captivated the entire family, Dad, especially, because he loved opera and often sang arias while shaving in the morning. He made a game out of presenting Hartley with pieces of music that Hartley would toss off as though they were trifles and then improvise around them, Dad calling out composers as though he were at a square dance. Harpo and Jenny were entranced, particularly when Hartley composed improvisations of his own around their personalities. For Harpo, he brought in staccato, Stravinsky-like riffs, capturing perfectly Harpo's jerky, Chaplinesque way of moving. For Jenny, the composition became graceful, full of rippling arpeggios and Mozartean trills in the treble that made us all laugh.

Between Hartley and Mrs. Loring, my interest in music grew by giant steps. Hartley told me that he thought he was Sergei Rachmaninoff reincarnated because both he and the composer had been born on the same day, they had the same kind of wide bridge in their hands with bony, knobby fingers, and Hartley thought the boy Rachmaninoff in photographs resembled Hartley himself. Hartley's ambition was to become a concert pianist and play Rachmaninoff's *Etudes Tableaux*. We decided that I should aim for Lizst because he had a brilliant piano technique, which I aspired to, and often dramatized his concerts by breaking a string or two at the piano to shock his audiences. I told Hartley I had done this years ago, as though I had invented it, not Lizst.

In July, Hartley and his watchful grandmother left. Mrs. Loring and I went to the ferryboat to wave them off, back to the simple life in Vermont with "Farmer Joe," as she called her husband, for Grandmother, and the mysteries of Philadelphia in the fall and winter for Hartley when both his grandparents would be free to travel with him.

Mrs. Loring was very pleased with my progress and now decided to take on a second pupil in September. Wouldn't you know, Jenny had convinced my parents that the cello was too difficult for her, that piano was what she had really wanted to learn all along. I knew Harpo would be on the bandwagon also in a year or two. I considered telling Mrs. Loring that Jenny listened to rock and roll with her friends and had a crush on some fool named Ringo Starr who played with the Beatles, but I decided not to, because Jenny could have reported, if she wanted to, that she heard me trying out my own compositions, *after* I had finished practicing, of course.

I had a new role model in my life now. I wanted to be like Hartley. I, too, would become a concert pianist and surprise everybody in Moscow, just as Van Cliburn had done.

When September came, regular school began too, but I found that I was beginning the academic year with a much more serious purpose. I no longer asked time-wasting, frivolous questions in class. I wanted to get this school business squared away as soon as possible so that I could get home and practice on the piano. I passed up my usual assignment as left end in our fall football games, the presidency of the stamp club, my exalted status as the giant brain in the geology club, my lackey job at Ben Whitefield's ferry pier, in favor of music. I had by now already conquered Chopin's "Etude in E-flat" and was struggling with Massenet's "Aragonaise" and Christian Sinding's "Rustle of Spring," showier pieces which would demonstrate my new technique and dexterity, not bad for four months' work, I thought.

One Saturday, near the end of the month, I was preparing to leave for my lesson when I noticed the wind acting up and the ocean boiling up on the rocks below our place. "What's the weather report?" I asked Mom.

"Small craft warnings," she said. "Why?"

"Looks cloudy out," I said.

"You're right," she said, looking out her bedroom window upstairs. "I'll call Herman at the weather station." In a minute she called down, "Take your umbrella and your slicker. Herman says the tail end of that hurricane is whipping up off the Cape, but we're supposed to be all right."

"Okay," I said. "See you later."

"Jenny and I are going in to town," Mom said. "May is doing my hair and Jenny's going to visit Elizabeth Presser."

"I'll be home later. I'm playing "Rustle of Spring" for her today."

"Good luck," Mom called down. "Get a gold star." She laughed. I didn't think it was so funny. I had worked hard enough on the fingering on that piece to earn ten gold stars.

I was early so I took the long way via Cliff Road to Mrs. Loring's house, that delightful Spanish villa that had gotten built because Mr. Loring had wanted to move to Florida or Santa Barbara and Mrs. Loring would live no place but New England. So that when Mr. Loring was assigned to the post of Chief Agronomist for the entire Maine coast, they compromised and built themselves "something worthy of the Costa del Sol," as Mr. Loring put it to me.

I thought the Lorings were wonderfully quirky people and I felt warm and happy as I thought about them while walking to what I assumed would be a routine lesson that day. The sea and sky were mixing together so that a fine spindrift from the waves kissed my face occasionally, but the surf crashing on rocks below got me right in the pit of the stomach with its booming sound. The wind was agitated, capricious, I noticed, frightening at times. The ocean had already turned a hard green and grey. Unseen bell buoys clanked out their mournful sounds in the distance, a bad omen, I thought. I saw no more seagulls cutting through the skies. "Windy out," I told Mrs. Loring. " But the tail end of that hurricane is going to miss us, Herman says."

"Just so long as it leaves us alone," she said. "Well, are we ready? Now, today, you were going to play "Rustle of Spring" all the way through for the first time. Are your hands warmed up yet?"

I felt good playing it. I may have hesitated at the beginning, as I sometimes did, but, otherwise, I thought I played it very well.

This was at about 9:30 a.m. We were in the middle of discussing it, Mrs. Loring having decided that it didn't quite rate a gold star, but she would give it a bluebird instead, meaning it was a happy effort, when the telephone rang. Mrs.

Loring answered it, saying, "I see. No, it's not raining. I don't think it's necessary. Another half hour or so, I'd say. All right, goodbye." She hung up and sat down next to me at the piano. She appeared amused by the phone call. "That was your mother," she said. "She's worried about the storm. Wanted to pick you up. I think Mr. Sims in town got her all riled up. She said some sign had blown in his window."

"Really?" I said. "The window of the General Store?" This sounded good. Too bad I was missing some interesting action.

"Well, then, let's get back to business," she said. "Now this passage here really needs a more legato style. You are rushing it." She marked it with her pencil and I played it out for her, slower this time, letting my fingers stick to the keys as though glue was on them, which is what I thought she meant by legato.

"That's better. Gieseking would never have rushed this."

Walter Gieseking and Dame Myra Hess were her two favorite pianists. However they would have done it was the best way .

"Let me see what your left hand does with this bass passage," she said, indicating a roll in the bass clef. I played it out for her.

"I thought so," she said. "You've got to roll it over your wrist more, from left to right." She demonstrated in the air. "Otherwise you are forcing it and straining your wrist."

Suddenly, through the whining wind outside I could hear the church bells ringing three times in succession, then a repeat. That means trouble on our island. We're fifteen miles out from the mainland, only six miles long and two and a half miles across, and at times like this you feel vulnerable and isolated. Electricity fails, wires go down, shutters are pulled tight on houses, people scurry inside and hunker down close to the earth, hoping they'll be spared whatever the weather brings. "Listen," I said.

She opened the door a crack, pointing her jaw toward the weather and closed her eyes. "That's St. Anthony's," she said. "You can't hear our church in a wind like this." She walked over and looked out a window to see if the sky looked different to the east. "It is acting up a bit. Well, never mind. Let me hear that bass roll again." I repeated it.

After about twenty minutes, a car pulled up outside, and there was a knock at the door. To my surprise it was my mother, very flustered and excited, with a wide-eyed Harpo and Jenny in tow. Mrs. Loring held them at the door, not admitting them, not inviting me to get up from the piano bench. I could see them exchanging a hurried conversation; I could watch Harpo and Jenny as though they were in some silent movie, but I couldn't make out what anybody was saying. Mrs. Loring finally closed the door and came back to the piano. The car pulled out and went away.

"Your mother is worried," Mrs. Loring told me. "It seems we may get the tail end of that hurricane after all, but not until tonight. I told her you hadn't finished your lesson. I don't know why she's so worried. Just because a few signs are down."

"Did she mention the church bells?" I asked.

"Oh, yes. It seems they've asked the residents of the Lighthouse Hill section to gather in St. Anthony's as a precaution. It's made of brick."

"But what about our place?" I said. "It's made of wood."

"The Cobbs Point section is better protected, I'm sure," said Mrs. Loring. "The Hill is the most vulnerable." She looked out the window. "Oh, it *is* raining now. Well, you brought your umbrella and raincoat, didn't you?"

"Yes."

"This will delay Mr. Loring's return. He was over in Bangor at that horticultural convention." She picked up the phone, listened, got no response. She clicked it impatiently. "Phone's out," she said.

"I thought that hurricane was supposed to pass us by," I said, aware that my voice was quavering since I'd been prisoned off from my family.

"It will head out to sea eventually," she said. "They always veer to the East when they get up this far."

We went back to my lesson, but neither of us had our hearts in it now.

Neither of us would admit that we were scared. Finally, she bundled me up, went outside with me to test the winds, which, we both agreed, were pretty strong, but not the worst we had seen, and I struck out. I decided to go back the way I had come, the longer way along the higher but surer Cliff Road. When I reached the turn on to it at Diablo Point on the north end of the island, I couldn't believe the monstrous waves crashing down below. The sky now just disappeared into the water with the rain slanting down so much and the clouds tearing by as though they were only ten feet over my head. I could feel the wind pushing me and making me slide on the slippery road. I thought I had better try the shortcut down by Hansford Smith's farm and cut through Driscoll's farm, bringing me out by Cobbs Woods and then across their access road to where their property met ours on the Point.

I was already thoroughly soaked and shivering. The umbrella became a cane and a prod for me to poke my way along with. One couldn't possibly think of opening up an umbrella in this storm. The Smiths had pulled the shutters closed on their house and there was no sign of any activity at all at Driscoll's, not even any lights, since it was now as dark as early evening, Was the electricity out, too, I wondered? Still we all had candles and oil lamps for emergencies just like these, and I knew the Cobbs had their own private generator, but they were only here in the summer anyway.

I began to get really scared, but I didn't have time to worry about it since surviving and getting home were all I could struggle with now. And it was taking every ounce of my strength. I pictured Harpo's and Jenny's tense faces straining at the window, looking for me to appear in the road that leads to the house. Then I worried that the house itself might have been blown away into the sea with all my family drowned.

I hustled now, entering the dark pine woods belonging to the Cobbs. Trees were down, I could see that, and more were crashing all around me. Luckily, I just pushed through, not stopping, not really realizing how dangerous this was when, suddenly, I felt a quick, dull blow to my head and I pitched forward, landing on a spongy bed of wet pine needles. I must have been knocked out for a few seconds, or minutes, I never knew which, because when I came to, all I was aware of was the pungent smell of wet piney earth, a tremendous roaring in the trees above me, punctuated by sharp cracks of falling limbs and trees, and the high whining sound of something that sounded peculiarly like a theremin playing Sinding's "Rustle of Spring" at a very fast clip.

I shook myself, realized who I was, where I was, and what I wanted, got to my feet, and pushed through to the end of the woods where I recognized the road to the Cobb mansion which was gleaming white, low and solid in the distance, as usual. Thank God, that had survived, I thought. The light was better now because I was out in the open, and I tore across their lawn and out to the field that adjoined our field.

I saw a dull yellow glow through the rain and darkness, lunged toward it, and fell in a crying heap into the arms of my mother and Dad who had been out in the rain in his yellow Gloucester slicker and who had been desperately flashing around a red emergency lantern looking for me. A white-faced Harpo and a solicitous Jenny were alternately trying to feed me hot cocoa, a glass of water, and supply me with tales about the adventures they had had in the car on the road. My mother made me take off all my clothes, and then she rubbed me with Turkish towels, put me into my pajamas and bathrobe and tucked me into bed on the living room couch where all the family was huddled against the terrible storm outside. I decided on that day that music was not worth dying for; only my family was.

It was four days before we learned the full extent of the damage and a week before we got electricity and the telephone back. The day after the storm, Sunday, everybody was still assessing personal property damage while the volunteer firemen and fishermen checked places on the island to see what had been lost. The port had been hit the worst with two of the Kniepper children placed under Dr. Carter's care because of broken bones and lacerations suffered when their family's house collapsed at the same time a section of the pier did, taking with it Ben Whitefield's Port Clyde Ferry Office. Fifteen boats were also sunk, numerous trees and signs blew down, and Old Sims was mad as a hornet about that broken plate glass window in his store.

On Lighthouse Hill, several big trees were down across the road near the cemetery, and one landed squarely on the Hoovers' summer home, smashing in the roof and the front porch. Cobbs Point survived intact, as did the north end of the island. But the first boat over from the mainland Monday morning brought news of scattered damage from other coastal communities. They said Mt. Desert and Bar Harbor had escaped because the storm apparently slapped inland near us but then turned sharply and veered out in a northeasterly direction toward Cape Sable and Nova Scotia.

Old Sims claimed the meteorologists were fakers anyway. He said he knew the eye of the hurricane went right over us because he said there was a deathly calm for about twenty minutes when there was no sound at all. He said he was listening. His son and daughter-in-law, with whom he lived, swore he was right. But Ben Whitefield told Dad that Old Sims couldn't hear a damn thing anyway and that he could barely see, either.

At first, my mother was quite annoyed with Mrs. Loring for not releasing me from my piano lesson, but Dad calmed her by saying, "How did she know how serious it was? She was only doing what she thought best—carrying on with the lesson." Later, Mother decided she'd better go to church to get more news. When she returned she reported that Mrs.

Loring had shown up and that she had said she had no idea of the power of that thing and that she was worried sick thinking about my going home right in the middle of it. I basked in the family's sympathy for one day, at least.

There was no school Monday, Tuesday, or Wednesday. Things got back to normal again only on Thursday. I used the time at home to practice that frustrating "Rustle of Spring." I did lots of limbering-up exercises for my fingers by playing those Hanon workouts over and over. On Saturday, I showed up at Mrs. Loring's at the usual time for my lesson.

"Goodness," said Mrs. Loring when she opened the door to admit me. "That *was* quite a storm, wasn't it?"

"Any word from Mr. Loring?" I asked.

"He's here," she said. "He came over on the ferry Tuesday morning." She indicated the other room where Mr. Loring sat in his chair studying the music that he would be singing in church next Sunday.

I looked into the room. "Hello," I said.

He smiled. "Hello," he replied. "Heard you had quite a time with the storm on Saturday. Mrs. Loring told me how you stuck it out."

"We thought it would pass us by," I said.

"They're tricky, those hurricanes," he said. "Can't tell what they'll do. I remember one, way back before you were born, raised a lot of hell around here."

"Patrick has almost conquered "Rustle of Spring," Mrs. Loring said to him.

"I think I've got it now," I said.

"Let's get to the piano then," said Mrs. Loring, carefully putting the rubber mat under our feet. "Now, then, I want to go over that one passage with you first. Did you get a chance to work out the fingering?"

"Yes," I said, playing the passage deftly.

"Good," she said. "Run through a few of those Hanon exercises to warm up your fingers, and, then, let's hear it."

She got up, faded back to the easy chair in the corner, and waited until I had finished chasing up and down the scale.

"Go ahead," she said, giving the signal. I knew she was behind me, listening carefully, her #2 pencil poised in the air over her notepad. I knew Mr. Loring was sunk into his chair, concentrating on hearing his inner tenor voice singing, but probably, also, hearing what I was playing. I thought of Hartley's sunny personality, overlarge for this Spartan room, and his peppery grandmother shouting out commands from the dining room. I thought of Mrs. Loring's Calvinistic God looking down in impassive observation of me.

Suddenly, I felt right at home here. I know this place, I said. No need to be afraid. I'm right at home. The old upright didn't look so formidable to me anymore. It was something I could look straight in the eye and not back down from. I could stare it down with ease now. I played "Rustle of Spring" with enormous gusto and authority, modulating it and infusing it with economical restraint, praise be to Gieseking and Hess. When I finished, Mrs. Loring said nothing, but her hand loomed authoritatively in front of the music on the piano. She planted a gold star there. I looked up at her and smiled. She seemed very pleased.

When I got home, Jenny came rushing at me, shouting, "Did you hear they're estimating close to a million dollars damage?"

"Don't bother me, Jenny," I said. "I've got to get to the piano."

Jenny looked hurt. I flew to the piano and launched into "Rustle of Spring." The hot wing of genius could not be stopped in full flight. Dad peered into the room. He must have looked from Jenny to me. I heard him say, "Ah, youth, ah, art." That was always the best thing about my father: His perfect understanding. He knew I was not to be done in by a mere hurricane. It would show up in my next composition, marked *molto agitato tempestuoso*. Leopold Mozart must have felt the same way about his son.

HARPO INAMORATO

I was coming down the stairs, but I paused in mid-flight, frozen, fascinated, because Harpo was on the phone, giving directions, and I always like to hear exactly how people give directions; it reveals an awful lot about them, I think. I can tell Harpo is talking to a woman because he's using that I'm-so-in-command kind of voice that comes off as overly patronizing and disaster-laden, especially from Harpo, because, typically, he's underestimating the common sense of the person to whom he's giving this walking-on-eggs treatment.

"If you do decide to come," I hear him say, "here's how you get here. Turn off Route 95 as soon as possible after Wiscasset and take old Route 1 north about twenty miles until you reach East Harmony, which is way out on a peninsula that gets narrower as you go out into Penobscot Bay. Once in town, turn right at the Congo church and you'll find yourself on Sorrowful Pond Road. Keep on for about eight miles until you come to that dark Swedish drink on the left. . . Because it's dark brown like most Swedish lakes . . . Never mind that the sign says 'Pleasant Lake.' That's the result of the East Harmony Citizens' Committee who gave it that name for the sake of the summer tourists. At the end of Sorrowful Pond, hang a quick right at the white farmhouse where the sign reads 'Peg's Eggs,' and then go exactly three and a half miles downhill--yes, it's a dirt road--to the boat landing. Be sure you get there at 10:00 a.m. sharp. That is the only morning run over to the island. Thomas Oates operates the ferry there. Tell him you're coming to see me and he'll see that you get on the right boat. There's another one out to Monhegan Island." Harpo turned to glare at me. "What are you looking at?" he snarled.

"Just recording all that important information," I said. "Who's coming? Princess Grace?"

"Patrick, Mom said you'd be no trouble. I hope that's true."

"What's her name again?" I asked.

"Maria Gabriela," said Harpo.

"*Grazie*," I said. "*La Princessa Maria Gabriela di Vicenza*, I presume."

"*Torino*," said Harpo.

"Resident of the elegant *Strada di Superga*, I suppose," said I, bowing in my most theatrical manner.

"Mom," yelled out Harpo. "Patrick's starting again!"

"No, I'm not," I said, heading out the door. "I'll leave you and Mom to your obsessive-compulsive housecleaning for your Radcliffe friend. And I'll be a perfect gentleman. *Ciao*, Harpino. See you later, Yank."

I suppose this has been going on since the first day Harpo was born. I was too young to know much about the whole ritual of birth and what a lowly sibling was expected to do. All I knew was that my mother had been gone over to the mainland for more than a week. Ben Whitefield had ferried her over somewhere to a hospital where Harpo had been born. She talked with me on the telephone. "You have a new brother," she said.

"I don't want a new brother," I replied. "Get home here right away." What did I need with a brother? We already had Jenny who could hardly contain her happiness. "The new baby will be my new baby," she told me menacingly. Big deal! She was welcome to him, I thought. The notion of two people to boss me around now was too much!

The new baby was originally named Henry, after my grandfather Curtis, but he never got called that. They say my father took one look at him in the hospital with that great mop of hair he had and that sappy drunken smile and called him Harpo in honor of the great comedian. My interest perked up considerably when I was told that someone named Harpo was coming home with my mother. We waited anxiously for the boat to push through the fog. I remember straining my eyes expecting to see Harpo Marx, Junior, but, to my disappointment, all I saw was a sleeping, red-faced doll with a bonnet on its head, no less—a little mummy wrapped up in several light blue blankets.

"That's no Harpo," I said to my father challengingly.

"Wait," said my father. "He has to grow into it." And, to Harpo's credit, he did.

I guess it never occurred to me that since Harpo was eight years younger than I, he would be the one to be bossed around by me. Jenny was two years older than I and always in cahoots with my grandmother in Boston, my aunts, and my three cousins about how superior women were to men, so it never dawned on me until he arrived how pliable and vulnerable Harpo would be. I would be the controller. And, indeed, despite what Jenny said, she lost interest in Harpo after a while, and it was I who used to take him for his walks in his carriage and his stroller. Later, Harpo would hang on to the tail of our German shepherd as we went down the road to visit Old Sims in his store or stopped to chat with red-nosed Mrs. Hamilton who had a parrot that yelled out "Give a damn, kiddo" and "Snuggle up, tootsie" to everybody who passed by. So, oddly enough, Harpo became my baby. I grew very protective about him and very proud of him when he smiled at people, as he often did, and batted his arms on the sides of his stroller, indicating his general happiness and satisfaction with the world. Harpo was well-liked, outgoing, and cheerful--all the things I never was, but could be, through him. So we got on fine.

Jenny was annoyingly smart in school, putting me to shame all the time. She was also a nice person. Teachers liked her. When I came along, replacing her in the Curtis lineup in school, teachers were always disappointed in me, both academically and socially. "Why do you hate me?" Miss Elsom asked me one day when she kept me after school.

"I don't hate you," I replied. "I hate Math." What a deplorable philosophy--numbers! Who cares about light years, or square roots, or stupid planes leaving Cleveland traveling at 240 miles per hour?

"You'll never amount to much, Patrick Curtis," was Miss Elsom's curt reply to me. So what? I had heard that same remark before. What did those people know about Hollywood, anyway, which was where I was heading, those dumb-cluck clam diggers on Spanish Island stuck way out in the trashbin Atlantic?

Fortunately, Harpo redeemed the family name when he hit school. Teachers adored him. He smiled and looked cute and was as bright as the Maine light on a good July day. They rushed him into French and Spanish and he became president of his class two years in a row. My mother always said she was so proud of Harpo and all his accomplishments. "You are the one I worry about, Patrick, " she said to me. "Jenny is the brain, Harpo the All-American, but you, Patrick, what are you?"

"I'm the poet and the philosopher-king," I said. I read that in a book about Plato, the dumb Greek homo, and it sounded pretty good so I shot it at Mom and anyone else who ever asked. That shut them all up, you can bet.

I was twenty-six, had been out of Dartmouth for five years, so, of course, I knew everything there was to know. Harpo was eighteen and just a beginning freshman, so, naturally, he had a lot to learn. He had always had a steady group of females interested in him. One of them, Betsy Mizell, had worshipped him since kindergarten. She was very quiet, not from wisdom, but from lack of it, yet her huge brown cow eyes followed everything Harpo did with complete understanding and love. We all assumed that Betsy and Harpo had become betrothed forever in the first grade. It was quite a shock to everybody when Harpo, who had joined the glee club at Dartmouth, met an attractive young woman who blew into Hanover one cold wintry night with the Radcliffe Glee Club and Tristan-und-Isolded her way into Harpo's heart. He announced well in advance that she would be coming over to the island for a weekend visit in the summer. "This must be really serious," said Jenny, who was always looking for relationships with marriage as the end result.

Maria Gabriela, on the other hand, sought out operatic partners. She had a lyric soprano voice, had studied music extensively, and found a richness in her native Italian opera. For her Santuzza, she required a Turridu. When she went to parties with camellias in her hair, as she frequently did, she would look in vain for an Alfredo over the drinks and canapés. When she was alone in her cold room in Cambridge, she sighed at the snow falling outside and yearned for a Rudolpho to bring her back to life again.

At Dartmouth, she was very pleased to meet up with Harpo at his fraternity house which hosted some of the Radcliffe singers. "*Mi chiamo Harpo*," he is alleged to have said to her when he was introduced, and she is said to have replied, "But you look more like Franco Corelli except for your blue eyes and your lighter hair." (Actually, I think he looked more like a sawed-off Art Garfunkel at that period, but you know what happens when two Romanticists collide).

Naturally, she found him fuzzy, cute, and quizzical. When she discovered that he had studied the violin and had a good tenor voice and that he had actually been to the Met in New York and seen *Rigoletto, La Boheme*, and *L'Elisir d'Amore*, the perfection of Harpo bowled her over completely. She invited him to Boston where she took him to Symphony Hall and the Isabella Stewart Gardner Museum, with promises of more Italian treasures to come in Venice and Milan, should he ever get there which she hoped would be soon. She was two years older than he was. He saw her as a dazzling European sophisticate and became her willing little Henry James initiate.

"You have many possibilities within," Maria Gabriela told him mysteriously. "I find you fascinating." You can just bet

Harpo loved that. Did that ever bolster his ego! "She finds me fascinating," he said to me earnestly, causing Jenny, my mother, and me to laugh immoderately.

Harpo's eyes flashed with anger. "She does, Patrick," he snapped. "And I am." I guess we helped him clinch the deal with his feelings.

Anyway, the great day arrived. Harpo stage-managed the whole production. Our father was banished to the mainland because he smoked a pack of Camels a day and Harpo didn't want the house to reek of tobacco, thus endangering La Gabriela's vocal cords. Mom and Harpo bought out all the air-freshener at Sims' store and then opened all the windows, letting ocean breezes zap through the house. Jenny was ordered to wear a yellow dress instead of her usual shorts, and I was commanded not to talk about my job at the boathouse or to ask Maria Gabriela if she wanted to go lobstering. Harpo chose the topics of conversation for me. They were: the weather, anything Italian (except pizza and other tomatoey subjects), good American writers, and anything in music (except rock, country, heavy metal, and hymns.) I asked Harpo if I could play *"Vissi d'Arte"* from *Tosca* on the piano, but, suspecting a trick, he vetoed it. I would have played it properly, as a tribute to lovers of their stature. Besides, I love the schmaltz of it all—"I lived for art, I lived for love"—tragic!

Maria Gabriela arrived as scheduled on the ten o'clock boat. You could tell Ben was impressed. He gave a little whistle as he helped her over the wobbly gangplank onto the pier and handed her over to Harpo. "Here's your lady, safe and sound," he said in his dry, ironic way. While they chatted on the pier and Harpo pointed out the major sights of the little port, Old Sims came out of his general store and stood there for a long time gawking at Harpo and Maria Gabriela. We would get his official critique later, I knew.

Mom, Jenny, and I lurked back a little, politely, waiting to be introduced. It seemed a long time before Harpo acknowledged us. "This is most of my family," he said super-casually. Jenny and I exchanged looks. We hardly expected to be high-hatted like this. Hadn't we cooperated?

But Maria Gabriela was beautiful--a warm and generous person. Her deep-set eyes took everything in quickly, and she seemed genuinely delighted with our spare little island. Of course she loved the way the light broke over everything, creating a vivid chiaroscuro . "Just like Italy," she said. "It is an artist's light. Do you paint?" she asked.

"Mom does," I said.

"Patrick does," said Jenny,.

"Jenny paints a little," Mom said.

"I did some water-colors once," said Harpo eagerly.

Maria Gabriela laughed. "Everyone should paint something this beautiful," she said. We all liked her at once.

We were really grateful that she liked the place. Not everyone does. We have had some guests who could hardly wait to get back to the mainland. "Don't you get bored with nothing to do out here everlastingly?" said my father's research partner when he came out for his one and only visit.

Mom had prepared a salmon and iced-tea luncheon for us on the deck overlooking the Atlantic pulsing lazily onto the rocks down below. I discussed the weather at great length, like some "hopped-up meteorologist," as Jenny put it, plus I threw in Orvieto, Siena, and Monte Cassino, since I had bicycled through Italy two summers ago. Even Harpo was impressed with what I had gotten out of the trip. Maria Gabriela wanted suggestions for a corresponding bicycle trip in the United States. We recommended California.

At lunch that day, Harpo learned something about Maria Gabriela that he hadn't known before. "Yes, I am diabetic," she had said. "It is not a problem. I control it well. Can we please go see some boats now? Yes?" I let Harpo walk her down to the boathouse. Jenny and I helped Mom clean up the table and kitchen. It took us all of eight minutes. We didn't have much to say to one another.

Maria Gabriela came only once more to the island, exactly one year later. She seemed perilously thin to me then, and Harpo said she had had some rough times with her health, with her eyes especially. He was very caring and careful with her, as were all of us, but one could see it coming the way one could predict the ending of one of her beloved Italian operas.

When Harpo would call from Hanover, we gradually less and less asked about Maria Gabriela. Inevitability was the silent beast in the middle of our conversations. Harpo made at least one weekend trip to Cambridge that we know of, but one day he called and said that Maria Gabriela had gone blind and that she was in Peter Bent Brigham Hospital. A month later he called us again and told us that Maria Gabriela had died and that he would be going down to Cambridge for a memorial service. We sent a bouquet of flowers and wrote out a cheque to be given for diabetes research.

When Harpo came home for spring break, he seemed so serious. He talked about school and said he had decided to try pre-med. Where was the happy-go-lucky charmer, I wondered? I tried to lighten up things for him at home, but nothing worked. "He'll get over it," Jenny said to me. And he did, eventually. He flunked out of Dartmouth and went into the army and was sent off to Viet Nam. For Harpo, the smiler, the comedy had ended just as it had for Canio in *I Pagliacci*.

THE DISCOVERY OF AUSTRALIA

The one thing on earth Jellico was certain he was good at was keeping secrets. He had promised Esdra he wouldn't tell anyone about their frequent daytime sorties to the old Patten cemetery tucked away high up on Lighthouse Hill, and he didn't. Esdra had convinced him that if word got out there would be hordes of tourists descending on the bone orchard for the same reason they went there: to picnic. And Esdra reminded him that she and Jellico were orphans, marooned forever on Spanish Island in the cold Atlantic, and that they couldn't ever expect an ounce of sympathy from their clam-digger neighbors if they were caught poking around the old relics pressing down the stiffs. So Jellico wisely kept his mouth shut.

Jellico was ten, a reasonably well-adjusted personality with an equable disposition. Teachers liked to use the adjectives "reliable" and "dependable" in describing him to others. His good friend was Marco Quatraro. Marco was Italian, but Jellico thought that he and Esdra were probably Greek. Their last name was Lamos. Esdra told Jellico that there were a lot of Greeks living in Saco on the mainland, if only they could ever get over there to ask a few significant questions. Both had tried unsuccessfully to find out something about their background. Mrs. Hamilton, with whom they lived, was a reluctant dragon about the past, seeming to believe that it was none of their business, she was responsible for them, always had been, and that was that. They knew there was something mysterious about their origins, and, Esdra, at least, made their difference into a virtue that pointed up their uniqueness. Once, some of Esdra's classmates had sneered at Esdra and Jellico and called them gypsies. Esdra looked up gypsies in the encyclopedia and told Jellico that yes, maybe they were gypsies from Greece who had migrated there from the deepest recesses of the Caucasus Mountains. Esdra said she rather liked being Greek and a gypsy. She told Jellico that being set apart made one more interesting. Jellico didn't much care, but Esdra loved being a unicorn.

Jellico was no mystery to his friend Marco. Marco called Jellico "Jellybean" because that's what Jellico had thought his name was when they were in kindergarten together. So the nickname stuck.

"Jellybean," asked Marco when the two boys were walking home after school, "Why do you let your sister push you around like that?"

"She doesn't," said Jellico.

"She bopped right into the cafeteria today and pulled you out of line. How come?"

"We had to go someplace."

"Oh, yeah, like when did you eat lunch?"

"I ate it," Jellico replied testily.

"How come Matt Howard saw you and Esdra wandering around the old bone orchard when you should have been here?"

"So what?" said Jellico. "A person can go where he wants to, can't he?"

"Your sister is real strange. You know that, Jellybean?"

"She isn't. She plays the violin, that's all."

"I don't mean that. That's no excuse. Look at me. I play the French horn, and I'm not strange."

"She practices more than you, that's all. Shut up about my sister, won't you?"

Just then Jellico caught sight of Esdra racing down the road after the two boys. Why does she have to run like that, thought Jellico? She looks like the Wicked Witch of the West outrunning the cyclone. Maybe Marco's right about her.

"Wait up," Esdra demanded. The two boys stopped and stared, wondering what she wanted.

"Please take these books home for me, Jellico," she said. "I've got some shopping to do." Her olive eyes were bright with the promise of a secret to share later.

"Were you and Jellybean out riling up the holy ghosts again?" asked Marco.

"What?" said Esdra.

"Today at noon. Matt Howard saw you and Jellybean."

Esdra shot a quick glance at Jellico. He rolled his eyes heavenward and shook his head no.

"You know something?" Esdra said to Marco. "You and Matt Howard are two of the nosiest creeps around." She handed her books to Jellico. "See you later. Don't forget." Then she ran on ahead of them.

Marco thumbed his nose at her retreating figure, and then, for good measure, gave her the arm. Jellico said nothing.

"I hate her," Marco blurted out. "She is damn peculiar."

"Why don't you shut up?" suggested Jellico.

"Glad she's not my sister," said Marco. "Boy, do I feel sorry for you."

"So what?" said Jellico.

"My mother thinks she's peculiar, too," Marco added to clinch his argument.

"Who cares?" said Jellico. "You're more of a pain in the butt to me, Marco. You're worse than Esdra, always bugging me about her."

"Hey, listen," said Marco, changing the subject when he noticed Jellico becoming really angry now. "I want to stop by the store. Let's see if Sims has gotten in those new comics yet."

"Sure," said Jellico. "Big deal, Marco. Comics!"

Whenever Jellico thought about it, which was often, he always concluded that Marco might be right. Esdra was kind of odd. For years, Jellico hadn't even been sure she was his sister. He thought she was a baby-sitter or Mrs. Hamilton's half-mad daughter. Funny the way Esdra was just a kind of extension of the house to him, living way up on the third floor, all by herself, where she had fashioned a bizarre studio, a great bird's nest in the attic. She had flung up a collection of old fringed shawls onto the rafters and distributed a couple of music stands, stacks of music, books, old pictures, and a rickety wooden artist's easel with canvases-in-progress around. She slept in an L. L. Bean summer hammock, slung up between the beams, and had no curtains on her single window which had a gorgeous view right down to the port and straight across the water to the mainland, which could easily be seen on a clear day.

Esdra was almost fourteen, but she sometimes felt ancient with all the responsibilities assailing her. She was annoyed that Mrs. Hamilton always appealed to the reasonable, the logical in her, forcing her to be aware that a foster mother, not a real one, was doing big favors in life for Esdra and Jellico every day of their lives. What made it endurable was that Esdra felt she and Jellico were only temporarily residing here and that there would be, in the future, a journey they would have to make to get where they truly belonged. It was like a story that she knew would unfold properly one day so that the two little orphans of the storm could live happily ever after.

Jellico was like her own child, she knew that, gladly assuming the role of the missing mother. Mrs. Hamilton could never play that part since she was an isolated, cold ruin of a castle surrounded by a moat of civility. Mrs. Hamilton was English by birth and upbringing, with sets of complicated rules that were incomprehensible. Always at four o'clock in the afternoon Mrs. Hamilton prepared her small pot of tea, and then at seven sharp came sherry, followed by dinner, which had to be eaten at the table, complete with no elbows on the table, napkins spread out carefully on the lap, and no dismissals until everyone had finished. Mrs. Hamilton had three rooms in the house which were reserved for paying guests in the summer season. Sometimes Esdra felt that she and Jellico were simply live-in help with tedious chores to do everlastingly for the benefit of the guests. The brightest spot at home, in Esdra's eyes, was Mrs. Hamilton's parrot, Malocchio, who sat in the front entryway screaming out salty comments to all who entered or departed from the house

Whenever Esdra tried to press Mrs. Hamilton about her origins, the woman would try to deflect her with humor or appeals to her sense of duty. "Oh, dear, now you know you and Jellico are my favorite permanent guests. I'm so lucky to have you here. All I want is that you do well in school and make something of yourselves. You know how proud I am of you both!"

Jellico, on the other hand, thought of his sister as a mixed blessing. She bossed him around even more than Mrs. Hamilton, but not so much as Marco, yet he knew Esdra was a special link to another world of which he was only remotely aware. She was dreamy and kind of lost in herself, he thought. She would sometimes put tapes into her tape recorder and do strange dances in her attic hideaway. Once in a while she would sing songs of her own invention. He had to smile because it sounded more like moaning than great art. She also painted pictures and wrote poems. She wrote one about him once and read it aloud to him. He remembered one line from it:

"He traveled far,
Yet never saw a distant land."

She told him it meant that he had a lot of inner resources. She said he would never have to depend on friends like Marco, that he could read, write, paint, sing, dance, play, and make up a whole world around himself, if he chose to. She said that's what she did. She claimed that was the secret of inner strength, and that's what he would always have. It sounded pretty good to Jellico. When he asked Marco if he believed in inner strength, Marco said no, the whole thing was a crock. But Marco didn't know everything, Jellico realized. He thought Esdra's system made a lot of sense, and that's all that really mattered.

The most restful place on earth, Esdra insisted, was right up here in the old Patten cemetery, now all filled up and forgotten by most, remembered only on certain veterans' days when a few representatives from the American Legion or Veterans of Foreign Wars would come up to plant a few flags or drop a few wreaths on selected graves. Otherwise, the small cemetery was green and quiet, tucked away from the road in a pine grove of tall sentinels keeping watch over the dead. The wind never roared through the place, but crooned softly in the branches up above. There was always a pool of warm sunlight in the center and a comforting stillness so that Esdra and Jellico could have their picnics in peace and tell stories about the people who inhabited the earthy tombs. Esdra maintained that, in places like these, spirits dwelled eternally. She and Jellico invented names for all these spirits, using as clues the bits of information they gleaned from each tombstone. Esdra was magical in her ability to weave stories from these hieroglyphics.

Jellico's favorite was Corliss Tichenour. It said on his tombstone:

CORLISS TICHENOUR
Aged Twelve
1823-1835
"The angel of the Lord came down
And Glory shone around."

Esdra explained to Jellico that it meant Corliss was taken away in an angelic flying saucer because he was too good for earth. He was forced to join the heavenly host almost against his will. Jellico resolved, when he heard this news, never to be too perfect, for fear of some jealous, ambitious angel snatching him away prematurely.

Esdra adopted a man named Colonel Samuel D. Patten. She made him an honorary great-grandfather. His stone mentioned "his singular distinction with the Union forces." Esdra told Jellico that he had been one of the leaders in swooping down on the evil South during the Civil War. She wove splendid stories about all the battles he had been in and all the wives he had had, especially his last one, the beautiful Zenobia Beaulieu, whom he had met in Charleston and who had instantly fallen in love with this conquering enemy because he was so handsome and impulsive. Esdra would pluck little rambler roses from Mrs. Hamilton's hedge and place them tenderly at Zenobia's grave. Her stone read:

ZENOBIA B. PATTEN
April 12, 1842--January 1, 1880
"Sweet Love Remembered"

Esdra said the worst thing that ever happened to poor Zenobia was when Colonel Patten took her away from her Southern plantation and brought her up to Maine. He had been a lumber merchant in western Maine and had made his summer home here on Spanish Island.

"Zenobia hated it here," Esdra solemnly told Jellico. "She longed for her home, for her brothers and sisters. She felt this island was uncivilized. She couldn't stand the people."

"Why didn't she just leave?" asked Jellico.

"Oh, she couldn't do that," said Esdra. "The Colonel wouldn't hear of it. Besides, they had ten kids."

"Ten?" said Jellico.

"Yes," said Esdra, "and do you know who one of them was?"

"No."

"Our grandfather."

"How do you know all this?"

"There are secret letters locked in the trunk in the attic. I haven't read them because she caught me at it, but I can tell from the stamps and the dates. There are lots of letters from a law firm. They tell the whole story about all this. Our grandfather died at sea, I believe, rounding Cape Horn, but he had married our grandmother, who lived in Australia, and they had our mother, Lila, who was a dancer and married Stathis, our father, who was Greek, until Mrs. Hamilton came along from Great Britain and stole us away from them."

"Are you sure, Esdra?"

"Positive. Cross my heart and hope to die. Our mother and father live in Australia, deep in the outback somewhere, and have millions of sheep. They are tremendously rich. If only we could get to them, Jellico."

"Why did Mrs. Hamilton kidnap us?"

"She was our baby-sitter. She was supposed to be our English nanny, hired to bring us up properly, but instead she was furious that she had no kids of her own to lord it over, so she spirited us away on her husband's pirate ship to this dismal place. I know our mother and father are thinking of us at this very moment and praying that we'll return some day."

"Couldn't we ask somebody to help us? Would Ben help?"

"No. These traitors in Maine all protect her. She has some strong witchcraft power over them. Her parrot comes from the pirate ship. You've heard the weird things he says. Mr. Hamilton got rich selling little children into slavery. When he was alive, he stole runaways and innocent kids. They just disappeared suddenly one night, the way we did."

"Let's go ask Ben, anyway," urged Jellico, shuddering visibly from a sharp chill.

"Don't count on anybody for anything," said Esdra.

Ben Whitefield was busy mending some frayed ropes at the dock. "Hello there, Jellybean, Esdra," he greeted them.

"How much would it cost to go to Australia?" blurted out Jellico.

Ben was amused. Jellico had an intense, concentrated look on his face. "Depends," he replied. "You going by way of the sea or the air?"

"It doesn't matter," said Esdra. "Just how much?"

"Does matter. Quite a lot," said Ben, putting down his rope for a moment to consider the situation. "Air's much cheaper, I think. Take you a month and a half by ship, I'd figure."

"Have you ever been there?" asked Jellico.

"Nope. Fastest way is by air. Out of Boston, I'd guess. When you planning on leaving?" He smiled at the image of these two en route to Australia.

"We're not, necessarily," hemmed Esdra. "We just want an estimate."

"Australia is full of millionaires who live on sheep ranches and have all the . . . " ventured Jellico.

"Shut up, Jellico," interrupted Esdra. "About how much would it be for two persons?"

"Going and return?" asked Ben.

Jellico and Esdra exchanged looks. "Well, one way first," said Esdra.

"You get a better deal on round trip, I believe," said Ben. "I wouldn't go for less than $3000 if I were you. But I'm not, and I'm not planning to go in the near future, I can tell you that."

"Thanks, Ben," said Jellico.

"Thank you, Ben," said Esdra, pulling Jellico away with her.

Ben watched the two children walk toward home. Then he went into his office and phoned Mrs. Hamilton. "Hello, Grace? Ben Whitefield here. Jellybean and Esdra were just by, talking about Australia. . . No, planning on going there, I'd say. . . Okay . . . I just thought you might want to know. G'bye."

Grace Hamilton moved to the front window in the living room and pulled back the corner of the curtain so that she could see farther down the road to the rise where Esdra and Jellico would first appear on their way up from the port. She felt a little sick and ran her right forearm around her stomach, holding it in tightly as though to suppress the pain she felt there. She greatly feared a confrontation of this sort, but could see it coming over the past year because Esdra had been pressing more and more, snooping into old letters in cardboard boxes in the attic, taking small clues and half-truths and obviously weaving them into desperate stories which led to the discovery of Australia. What Grace feared most, more than any loss to herself, was how destructive the news might be to Esdra and Jellico. Truth can destroy, Grace knew. She had seen it happen before. T. S. Eliot had written that "Humankind cannot bear very much reality," and Grace had found that precept accurate about her own life to this point.

As she looked out the window, she saw the treacherous fog slowly sneaking up the island, dragging in what would be an interminably long night for her. Over the rooftops to the harbor from her hill, she saw the ironically friendly flickering of lights coming on one by one, belying the denial of truth and light that suffused her own home. The dying fall of the foghorn ached in her ears, and she could hear the nervous clink-clank of a bell buoy in the harbor indicating the wind had picked up.

Grace forced herself to prepare her scenario. She remembered Suzanne Lamos, her first good friend in this country. She had known her when Grace and her husband, Jack, had opened up a restaurant in Portland back in the early days. Suzanne had worked for them as a waitress and borne two children out of wedlock. Grace had resolutely prevented Jack from firing Suzanne, whom she saw as a sweet, fragile soul. The shock of Grace's life came when Suzanne took a fatal overdose of pills one lean Christmas, willing a small amount of money and her children to Jack's care. Grace faced the terrible double truth about her husband and Suzanne in her stoical duty-bound way, but Jack later abandoned the unloving Grace and the kids, shipping out to Australia, leaving her to make her own way in what became a nightmare of a life, managing a B & B and trying to make a happy world for Esdra and Jellico. Now, they would blame her for hiding the truth, and she would lose them too. She could no longer make excuses. She was a denier of life, a betrayer.

The door opened suddenly and the two children plunged in, standing there.

"We have something to tell you," said Esdra, flinging her challenge to the English army.

THE SOUND OF SNOW FALLING

I am spending the night in an igloo that my father constructed out of great blocks of snow and ice on the front lawn. This is the same lawn that doubles as the edge of Sherwood Forest in the summer when I become Robin Hood and stand behind a big elm tree lancing passing enemy cars with plumed swamp grass spears gathered from the jungle by the Amazon River near our house.

We live on an island and so we always have very high humidity. This makes you feel colder in the winter and hotter in the summer no matter what the temperature. I was hoping for a lot of snow this winter, and, luckily, we got it. It is a wet snow, a packing snow, and it has been snowing now for almost two days straight. People call it an unusual snow. No school or anything. They couldn't even get the snow plow out. My father didn't go to work. The fire station blew its whistle at 7:00 a.m. which meant that there would be no school for anybody, even teachers, today. I finally got my wish, thank God.

So my father built this igloo. I helped, but he knows all about architecture and engineering and the way Eskimos make igloos and all, and so he made this wonderful ice palace for me. He called up to my room very early this morning while I was still asleep and said, "Robbie, if you want to have some fun, get your butt down here right away." You can bet I popped up fast to get downstairs to hear his plan. I intend to spend the night inside the igloo tonight. It is really very snug. I brought out a sandwich and some hot chocolate and had lunch there, but I have to admit my hands did get cold. I had to keep my gloves on, but they weren't much help. I think the fingertips had gotten too frozen from the extreme wetness of the snow.

I let Brian and David have a look at it. David wanted to go into it, but I was afraid he would stand up and wreck the whole thing, so I said no. David is a little young. They both really liked it, though. They said they wished their father would make them an igloo, but their father doesn't live with them anymore.

My sister, Penny, thinks it's stupid that I want to spend the night out here. She doesn't think I will go through with it. She never liked my tree house, either, and she wouldn't climb out the window at night when I made a bedsheet ladder so we could go on detective hunts in the neighborhood. The only thing she would do is when I made jet rockets out of cardboard, put them on my back and flew down the stairs to the living room and then flew from couch to chair to bench to chair and all around the room. She did that. She loves tumbling and calisthenics anyway. She thinks she is some kind of Olympic champion. What does she know?

I can't get over my father. I think he knows just about everything and can make just about anything. He made two large model boats for me and I raced them in model sailboat races over in Bangor and Portland. I won two "seconds" and one "third." Next spring I am hoping for a "first." My new sailboat is called "The Shamrock." My father built it as an exact replica of the famous one owned by Sir Thomas Lipton. We painted it green and white and we fly a little flag with a shamrock on it from the topmast. All my father's friends at the shipyard say he is the best at making model sailboats.

I read all about Eskimos in a book my father gave me. I can't believe they actually eat blubber. That's the one thing I don't like. I think it would be fun to fish through a hole in the ice, but I don't want anybody to give me blubber. I don't really think I like walruses either. They don't look trustworthy and they slither in a dangerous kind of way. That's a lot of weight behind them. I'd hate to bump into one of those on a dark night.

My best friend is not Brian or his little brother David. It's my cousin Daisy who lives not too far from our house and is just my age. Her mother and my father are brother and sister. Daisy is the only one who knows about the jungle and the Amazon River. Sure, other kids play there, but they don't know what they are really, and they don't ride horses.

I know our horses are only imaginary horses, but it doesn't matter. We are just practicing until we get our real ones. And we're going to get them soon. You see, my father and Daisy's mother's parents came to Maine from Canada, and their parents—I guess they are our grandparents—had a huge farm there and still have it even though the grandparents are dead. So we are planning to go there at least for the summer. My father's cousins run the farm, and, yes, there are horses there, and Daisy and I know that we will love the farm and we want to feed the chickens and milk the cows and do all that stuff. And, yes, I do know that it is all hard work. My mother is always saying, "Do you know how hard farmers work?" Yes, I know, Mother. I keep my eyes and ears open. I have seen farmers and fishermen on this island and on the mainland, and I have read many books on the subject and so has Daisy.

In the meantime Daisy came up with another plan. There are some very rich people who live up on Cobb's Point in what looks like a great marble palace, and they have a swimming pool and tennis courts, and stables, great long buildings that are hidden behind their house, and there actually is a track there and horses. We never knew that because you can't see anything from the road except the front of their house, but Daisy galloped her horse through the back of their property one time when she got off course, and she saw through the trees and bushes about four or five horses and a trainer there, and she galloped back over to my house and told me about it, so we galloped back and I couldn't believe my eyes.

The plan was that I would knock on their door and tell the people that Daisy and I were interested in horses and would they kindly let us have one. Daisy was afraid they wouldn't, but I thought they probably would because they had quite a few and we would take care of it and everything, probably better than they could, and it could stay in our garage, and I know my father would have kept the car out if I asked him to.

We went to their house at around noon. Rich people sleep late I know and I didn't want them to wake up all grumpy because I knew we would never get our horse if we disturbed their peace. A butler came and said, "Wait a moment," and then a lady with kind eyes and greyish hair came, and she listened and said, "Well, no, we can't let you have a horse, but anytime you would like to see the horses, just come and knock on the door." I think she thought we were funny. She called to a man to come and look at us. Well, I thought, so the plan failed. We still had the Canada idea going.

I wonder what Canada is like? I picture great rolling meadows. Lots of green. Blue skies with lots of clouds. White fences everywhere. Beautiful animals, great open spaces. Happy, smiling faces. No smoking cities. No screaming seagulls. Sometimes Daisy and I think we'd like to run away together to Canada. We get tired of this island. We don't like school.

My horse is named "Gladiator." Her horse is named "Miranda." After school we go home, change into our regular clothes and then go riding in the Brazilian jungle, up hill, down into little valleys, through the cattails, close to the Amazon itself, but we are always careful near the Amazon because it is tidal and the current is very swift. My father says it is really an inlet that sweeps out into the sea. We know it is treacherous. Jonathan Akerman drowned there. I remember the fire truck screaming and the volunteer firemen pushing up and down on Jonathan's chest. It didn't work. Daisy and I promised our parents we would never go into the water at the inlet or too near it. The jungle is dark, deep, and green. My father said it once was a granite quarry. We love to go exploring and to climb mountains there. There is even a ruin of a house that once was perched on the edge of the Sahara Desert where the old dry reservoir is. You can climb down into what was once the basement of this house. It looks like the photos of the ruins of Pompeii in our Ancient History book. But this is so much better. Sometimes I am Robin Hood and Daisy is Maid Marian. We may get married someday. Very few people know this about us.

Today, though, it is snowing even harder. Did you know that snow makes a kind of thudding sound when it comes down? It changes the appearance of everything. It makes uneven things even. There could be over a foot and a half of snow now. Our whole front lawn looks like the top of a cake. I would never know there is a road out there and another road that leads straight ahead to the jungle, the river, and Daisy's house. I don't even know where Daisy is today. The telephones are not working. I suppose she's stuck inside helping her mother the way Penny is doing in our house.

It's getting quite dark, kind of a bluish-black. I just saw my father look out the front window. He has the lights on in the living room and is building a fire in the fireplace in case the electricity goes out altogether. There is a yellow glow around him. It looks warm inside. I think my father is the best person on earth. I'm going to try to spend the night in my igloo. I'd like to show him I'm brave.

I am standing in my parents' bedroom looking out their front window. I had my twenty-first birthday yesterday, but what I am seeing is what I have seen all my life. It is February and the snow is falling so thick and heavy that I can't see very far down the road toward the inlet. Everything looks beautiful, of course, but everything has come to a stop. We are in a paralysis. The snowplow is not going, there is no telephone, no electricity, and very few people are trudging through the tricky snowdrifts. My father is not here. Just my mother, Penny, and I. My father is in the hospital in Rockland over on the mainland for the second time this year. His heart is giving out. I do not think he will make it. I am deeply upset, but I have been so busy at college and it took me such a long time to get here when they called me that I try not to think about things too much. Instead, I wait for the ferry to run again to take me over to him, and I look out the window into all this blueness and listen to the sound of snow falling.

The doctor called me yesterday about my father. He said it would be wise if I came first to the hospital in Rockland and then went over to the island because the weather was so bad. No let up. So I took the train from New Haven to Boston and then the bus up to Rockland. As soon as I got there I walked over to the hospital. My father was in a room with another man, also a father, also a heart patient. Just as I arrived, the other man's son arrived. He was about my age and also at college. We talked about our fathers and we talked to our fathers. What can you say? They had these great plastic cocoon-like oxygen tents around them. My father wanted a glass of water. I poured him one and reached into his tent with it. I felt so powerless in a world where I wanted to do much more for him, but I had to trust to the doctors and nurses. And I do trust them. I hope they will pull him through. I don't want to do or say anything that might upset him. I make small talk about how school is going. I joke that I don't really like New Haven, too many clothing shops, I can't figure out the library's cataloguing systen--things like that. I tell him about how I had to walk to the New Haven railroad station which looked as though it were set in some frozen Siberian tundra. I am aware that he is more interested in other matters. I read the desperation in his eyes; the sheet must come up a little higher, the bed should be lowered a little, why is the nurse so late with his medication? Did the doctor say anything to me? Why didn't my mother and sister come to the hospital with me? What does it say on the chart at the foot of the bed? Is it a good report, or not?

I stayed about forty minutes. I would have stayed longer, but my father closed his eyes and appeared to be sleeping. I thought it better to let him rest. I went out into the hall.

Richard, the other man's son, was leaving at the same time. We wished each other good luck. Our chances apparently are fifty-fifty, but we are sons and we cannot give up our fathers easily.

I got the last ferry over to the island before the snow closed it down. Now I am marooned and I feel the snow may just cover us over so that we will disappear from the earth forever. My mother and Penny are downstairs in the kitchen baking some toll house cookies. The warm aroma of chocolate drifts up to me. They are doing this to cheer me up, I know. They know how difficult it is for me even to speak. I look out the front window once more. There is a wind rising now, stirring up the snow, providing little vistas through which I can clearly see the whipped cream drifts on the front lawn where once my father built an igloo for me in which I could not make it through the night. Why did I fail him then? The unusual snow presses down around me so that it hurts. It closes me in, forcing me to see things that matter in a piercingly hard light.

There is an odd knocking at the door, someone pounding, insisting. My mother answers it. I can hear her voice and that of Ben Whitefield who runs the ferry service over to Port Clyde and East Harmony. He is saying something. The kitchen and downstairs hall go silent all of a sudden. A strange stillness freezes me to the bannister in the upstairs hall which I clung to when I first heard the knock. It is so quiet I can hear the dull thudding of the snow on the roof of our house. I can tell now from what my mother is saying that Richard has won and I have lost.

THE GAELIC BOY

His real name was Teilo Brychen, not Sean Mullally, (who was a guest of the Noons on the island at the same time), and he spoke Welsh, not Irish Gaelic. But these were the least of the lies spread about him during the spring he was on the island. He was thirteen years old, which they got right, and he spoke and understood English perfectly, which they wondered about, but never heard because he was a superb actor and chose not to say anything in English to anybody ever. He had his reasons.

When I first saw him, I was taken aback because of what I can only call his startling physical beauty. Perhaps a man like me is more sensitive to this particular quality in another male than a woman might be because it's so rare and unexpected. He looked like a delicate shepherd boy made of bisque which I had once seen on a plant stand in an antique shop in Boston. Yet his arms and legs were long and sinewy, indicative of greater strength than was apparent. He was fine-featured with deep-set blue eyes, high cheekbones, and a translucent porcelain complexion that made you doubt he could ever grow a beard or mustache. Colt-like, that's what he was. Awkward and graceful at the same time. Arresting. You had to look at him. He appeared to be aware of the attention he drew. He seemed almost to will it out of you.

He wasn't a native, that was certain. The entire state of Maine has never bred such a Gainsborough boy as he was. Our island boys are sturdier, rougher-looking. They hug the ground when they walk. They lean into the wind. This boy seemed to skip. His choreography was all air and fire. On this island we're all earth and water.

It's funny that I should still think about him at this late date. What I knew was very sketchy at the time—just glimpses of him at school or on the Cliff Road walking home—

and I have never been certain of just what I actually did overhear. Maybe I imagined some of it or made up parts of it. I told what I knew to Judge Herrick Williams at the hearing, but he appeared to dismiss my testimony as though all of it was just circumstantial, so maybe I never really heard anything important, but just had a feeling, a thought or two, that may have seemed pertinent, but, in reality, had no basis in fact.

To be truthful, Teilo Brychen wasn't even in my class at all. I taught physics in the Spanish Island high school, and, although he turned up in my class the first day, it was a mistake. He was supposed to be in physical education that period. The secretary's abbreviation wasn't clear to him on his schedule. He showed it to me, and I told him to go down to see the coach in the gymnasium. He never said a word, but smiled a "thanks" at me. That's when I noticed his unusual, ethereal appearance.

His homeroom teacher was Camilla Stefanik. Later, in the teachers' lounge, when I inquired, she told me he had come to the island with his mother, an actress, who had rented the Curtis home "July Blue" for the year, riding out a divorce from her Welsh movie producer husband. Camilla said the mother was a wild gypsy, all dark hair and angry eyes, who acted on the London stage. Camilla said her take on the situation was that Teilo was so angry with his mother for divorcing his father that he was rebelling against her and everything she wanted him to do, which was to hole up on our island for the year. Camilla said she thought Teilo brought on himself everything that happened to him. She said he and his mother were two of the most self-centered persons she had ever met. She told the judge of the tremendous inner tensions she felt between mother and son.

According to Camilla, Teilo read quietly in class, but wouldn't answer questions, which annoyed her at first because she could see the other students thought this was a great game, brinksmanship, with Teilo openly defying her authority, winning. Since Camilla had trouble maintaining discipline anyway, this was greatly disturbing to her. But soon she left Teilo alone when she saw that his sullen attitude extended also to the students, who soon moved from admiration to rejection to scorn, insisting that Teilo suffered from a superiority complex.

The trouble was and still is that Camilla equivocates. She'd say one thing about him at one time, and offer a different opinion at another. She admitted to me that she found Teilo fascinating, but then so did everybody. He simply was an enigma, a mysterious, disturbing presence that drove the whole island mad. Among normally reserved people, he was so remote that he was impossible to reach. Judge Williams couldn't ever find a single person who had anything but the most nebulous impressions about what Teilo Brychen did, said, or thought after school. In fact, most of the students and teachers interviewed, including me, had never heard Brychen utter a single word.

His mother, of course, was never heard from again after it happened. She left immediately after the hearing, apparently going directly back to London. Ben Whitefield said she left with a man who came over on a motor launch with two other men who helped her load up the boat with her belongings. Ben said he thought the man had an English accent, couldn't be sure, didn't talk with him. Grace Hamilton said about a year later she saw a show in London with a Drusilla Brychen in the cast. Grace said it was Shakespeare's *As You Like It* at the Barbican and that Drusilla Brychen played Audrey in it. Grace wasn't certain, of course, but she thought it was the same woman. That's all we know and all we ever heard about what happened to her. The same as with Teilo—very little information.

I developed a theory about the boy as soon as I heard what happened. For years, in Wales, Scotland, and Ireland there's been a movement toward nationalism, toward getting back to a culture that antedates the Anglo-Saxon invasion that brought in the English language. Those native Brits were Celts, their language was Gaelic, but the newer, dominant

English culture suppressed the language and the ancient religion. Around the beginning of the twentieth century, people on the islands in the Hebrides, on the coast of Wales, and in western Ireland, began not-so-quietly getting back to their roots, teaching Gaelic, changing signs--from "Queenstown" to "Cobh" in Ireland, for example--and, even though they may have been fighting a losing battle--a minority against a majority--their attempts to revive the ancient language were not without passion.

Teilo Brychen's divorced father was a producer or director of films, they said, from Cardiff, Wales, although nobody I ever met could even identify a single film by him. Since the boy was fluent in Gaelic and refused to speak English here on the island, I deduced that his father must have been one of those Welsh nationalist-linguists, engaged in making naturalistic semi-documentary films and that the boy was merely reflecting his father's attitude by insisting on Gaelic. Maybe the boy saw the absurdity or the futility of the position his father had taken and was just pushing it to an extreme in an unconscious move toward self-destruction. I don't know for certain, of course, but it made sense to me because I think that's what I would have done had I been in the same situation, with the same feelings.

The three boys that were involved with Teilo Brychen on that last day were an interesting lot when you think about them, as I had to do carefully before I told the judge my story. I knew all three of them quite well. Two had been students of mine in physics. I won't give away their last names here, but will use fictional names since I feel it is important to remain as impartial as one can in this case, there's been so much talk already. The smartest boy, an "A" student, I'll call Michael. He was tall, thin, blond, of Swedish background, I think. His father was a fisherman who married a Spanish Island woman whose family owned the big inn. Michael grew up working in the inn, lugging baggage, putting out garbage, peeling vegetables in the kitchen. He was conscientious and intelligent, but as he grew older I guess he realized how clever he was, how practical, and how he could turn that to his advantage. I noticed that, although he was quiet and low-key, he had a lot of intellectual power among the students. When he suggested something, it was pretty much accepted without question. I know some teachers who used to mention how sensible Michael was about all aspects of his life. In my physics lab, unlike other students, he did his experiments when they were supposed to be done. You got a minimum of complaining from him. It's not that he was resigned, or overly-determined, either. He just took a sane, rational approach. He was a pragmatist. That's what everybody said about him, I included.

Dennis, on the other hand, was a dark, ratty kid who grew a beard in high school as soon as he could. He had muddy brown eyes that rarely looked directly at you. You got the impression he was hiding his thoughts from you, concealing his motives, his true self always. He was openly manipulative, striking out, making emotional pleas for his point of view, which were not always heeded, but which instigated hot arguments. Sometimes these would come to blows. Several times after school I saw Dennis out of the corner of my eye, in the middle of scraps, once or twice where he was punching out some kid or being hit in return. Nothing serious, but he was a contentious kid, I'd say. He was the younger of two boys in his family, probably at a disadvantage, since Steve, his sibling, had been a star athlete in school, well-liked by everybody. But that was years ago before I taught at this school. I think there was about eleven years difference between the two boys.

Piggy Balls was what the third boy was called. His real name was Paul, but nobody ever called him that, even the teachers called him Piggy in class. He had one of those placid, well-balanced personalities you admire in the young. He just was so nice and polite that everybody couldn't help liking him. Naturally, he was not the swiftest student cerebrally, just a "C" student all the way through, I imagine, but wherever he was the sun just naturally shone. I never had him as a student, of course. Physics, I'm sure, would have been too overwhelming for him. He took a course in auto mechanics, instead, worked after school at the boatyard, where he was highly thought of. One of the reasons the hearing went the way it did, I feel, is that everybody loved Piggy Balls. Nobody could think him capable of any wrongdoing or lying.

I listened carefully to what he said at the hearing because he showed up at the scene after the other two were allegedly already on the rocks and Piggy had an overview that included them and Teilo in it. Piggy was a close friend of the other two, so if anything had been planned, premeditated, Piggy would have realized it. He was the most fluent in his testimony. You had the impression of complete candor. He appeared to tell it just as it happened, without any suggestion of guile on his part. What would he have to gain? After all, what he did say involved two of his closest friends and he wouldn't have wanted to incriminate them needlessly. But the problem was that Piggy was no more certain than the rest of us about what he thought he saw.

Dennis, on the other hand, was defensive, evasive it seemed to us. Judge Williams tried to find contradictions in his testimony, but couldn't really shake him. I think the boy was terribly nervous, also, under all that pressure. I noticed he kept exchanging looks with his mother who we all knew was torn apart by all the allegations. Her eyes were red and her son, Steve, put his arm around her as though holding her in, she looked so frail and thin. Michael's testimony was reticent, almost apologetic, few words. He said he was sorry it happened but he didn't feel guilty about it or responsible in any way. He said he just didn't know what happened.

Piggy Balls, the last to testify, said that he left school at 4:30 p.m. on that Friday. He said he noticed the sun had disappeared and that the clouds were closing in low and fast. The ocean was already roiled up, leading Piggy to believe, as most of us did, that a storm was brewing, a nor'easter. Normally, Piggy said, he would have gone directly to Cy

Young's boatyard, where he was due at 5:00 p.m., but he decided to go home first to get his schedule sheet which he had forgotten. He took a shortcut, because of the weather, that had him climbing on the boulders at the south end of the island, Cobb's Point, to the old Longpre place where his family's cottage was. He said as he edged his way along the top of the cliffs, he saw, or thought he saw, down below, Michael and Dennis in the middle distance, on some rocks, overlooking the dock at "July Blue" where Piggy said he caught a brief glimpse of Teilo Brychen standing there, bending over, looking into the sailboat tied up with the dinghy in back. Teilo appeared to be untying the dinghy from it. Piggy didn't see any more because the fog was coming in fast and he began to be afraid he couldn't make it, so decided to turn back. He said he called to Michael and Dennis, who appeared to him to be watching Teilo. He said they never responded to his call, but disappeared instead behind the boulders. Because of the thick fog he said he wasn't really sure he had seen them at all.

This is where I came in. I know for a fact that Michael and Dennis were together that afternoon, because as I went down to the restroom from class at about 3:00 p.m. that afternoon, I overheard the tail end of a conversation as the two of them passed me in the hall. I saw Dennis with an unusual, flushed look on his face and a tight smile, listening intently as Michael said with a kind of swagger: *"Bitheam,"* is what he said. It seemed as though it meant "Leave me alone." I didn't think much about it at the time because I didn't know what they were talking about, but when I thought about it later, I remembered that it sounded like a translation. Michael was giving Dennis information about what he thought something he had heard meant. And it wasn't French, German, or Spanish, but was it Gaelic? Was he repeating something Teilo Brychen had said?

At the hearing, the two boys didn't deny they had passed me in the hall and were talking, but they claimed they were talking about a movie they had seen over in Rockland. Four other boys stated they had seen the movie with them, so the judge said was I certain that was what I had heard and I had to admit that I couldn't be sure. You overhear little snippets of conversations out of context so that they never make sense at the time. A big problem we all had was that, after the fact, everybody had something he or she thought had been seen or heard, and it all seemed logical once you pegged it to a certain scenario. In fairness, I had to back down. I really don't know what the two boys were talking about.

Michael and Dennis both denied they were anywhere near the rocks that afternoon. They claimed that after school they went over to the general store to look at comic books. This was verified by Old Sims, as was their subsequent statement that they parted in front of the store to go their separate ways home. Sims said he saw Michael head down Front Street toward his home which is the last one on the right hand side. Michael's mother said she wasn't home at the time but that he called her on the phone at the inn to let her know he was home.

Dennis said he walked up Lighthouse Hill, passed the Hamilton home where the parrot was screaming at him, got to his home where he took a nap. His mother backed him up on this, but some of her neighbors disputed her claims, including Grace Hamilton who said that her parrot, Malocchio, wasn't out in his cage on the porch that afternoon and couldn't have screamed at Dennis. She said she had brought Malocchio into the house because of the approaching storm, and the Judge said, "Well, then, the parrot had been outside in his usual place in the porch at an earlier time." Grace had to admit he had been. She wasn't very clear on the time. She just made things worse, the more she talked.

The storm broke at 5:20 p.m. that day. The sky went dark and the wind whipped us good, about 45-50 miles an hour, I'd say. Three boats capsized in the harbor and the afternoon ferry from the mainland couldn't make its run. At "July Blue," the sailboat rode out the storm intact, but the dinghy broke off and slammed out to sea and wasn't found until a week later forty miles up the coast on the mainland. The rope that bound it to the sailboat was still on it, but the front starboard cleat where another rope had fastened it to the wharf was broken, probably from being pounded on the rocks.

Teilo Brychen's body was never found, never washed up on the mainland the way the dinghy did. It was a complete mystery whatever happened to that kid. People came up with various theories at first, like he was hiding, playing a cruel game to scare his mother into getting him off the island. Other ideas were that he disguised himself, went back to the mainland as an anonymous passenger. That has been tried before, successfully. Some said he committed suicide, knew that he could cover it up in the storm. Only a few thought he met with foul play, maybe pushed off shore without an oar by a person jealous of him or anxious to get even with him in some strange way.

I had those thoughts myself. I mean, it happened many years ago, and yet I still think about it and wonder. I noticed that the friendship among Michael, Dennis, and Piggy Balls seemed to dissolve forever after the event. Michael and Dennis remained close, but in less than a year Dennis and his mother moved away to California and, after high school, Michael went over to Orono to the university. Piggy still works at the boatyard. I can tell you the whole thing was the greatest puzzle we've ever had here on the island. I can still see that wraithlike creature Teilo threading his way through the other students on that first day of classes. I wonder who he was, what his presence meant to us on this island, what his disappearance signified? Or if it mattered at all? We just don't know, and I guess we never will. All of us are wary of and respect weather, tides, and accidents.

SUMNER OF THE SPANISH MAIN

It isn't easy to get to Sumner. You have to slide over stinking, seaweed-covered rocks and dodge whirling gulls screaming down at you and cracking clams ruthlessly. Then you have to climb up his haunted tower, reeking of wet cement and whitewash, mount clanking iron steps spiraling toward the lazy, revolving light at the top. There you might find Sumner with his red beard and far-away blue eyes, and if he's in a good mood, he may talk to you and tell you stories of his days in the merchant marine sailing to Spain, Africa, and Australia. Still, he is peculiar. Everybody on Spanish Island says that. He lives in the old lighthouse which doubles as a fire tower on our wooded, hilly island. He's just about the last of a breed these days, all the lighthouses being automated.

I'm only fourteen, but I've lived on this island, summers mostly, since I was born. Othertimes we live in Cambridge, Massachusetts, where my father teaches geology at Harvard University. But Maine is where my heart lies. It's my true home—all that pounding ocean, mysterious fog, and strange beings like Sumner, the Flying Dutchman of my life.

"He's an odd duck," says my mother. "He didn't get along with his own family. He's a loner, but he's a good fire warden, a good engineer. He helped us once with our generator when we had trouble. He knows a few things. But he has no friends."

No friends, I think. But he has eyes that see far out across the water. He tells about ancient wrecks, knows tides, currents, where the best lobsters lie hidden. He tells us boys these things sometimes. He intrigues me. I would like to be his one friend on earth. I decide to visit him alone one day so I can have him all to myself. He is the most fascinating person on this island.

One day in June the day is just perfect—that clear blue sky that brings out the kooky artists on the rocks, very little breeze, everything looking very smart and shiny. After school, I head toward the lighthouse, determined to probe the secret soul of Sumner. Luckily, he's in a perky mood. He's poring over a large scrapbook.

"Hello, Patrick," he greets me, "What brings you up here?"

"Just seems a nice day," I reply. "Wondered what you were doing."

Sumner flusters a little, I notice, closing the book. "This? Nothing much."

"What is it? What do you keep in it?"

"Just some correspondence. Letters."

"You get letters here?" I'm astonished. It's never occurred to me that anyone would ever write to Sumner or any giant in a tower. I thought they did everything by Morse code or telephone.

"Yes, I can write, too," Sumner says, smiling, making me feel ashamed I asked such a dumb question. He opens his book again and caresses a page with his hand.

"Who do you write to?" I ask, surprised at this tenderness in Sumner.

"My ladies."

"Excuse me?"

"My ladies," he repeats. "Look." He gestures for me to come and look closely at a page. The top of it is printed with the words "The White House." The letter is signed by the secretary to Mrs. Barbara Bush. The letter says something about Mrs. Bush's busy schedule but she will see what can be done. Sumner flips a page. I look. Here is a letter signed by Jacqueline Kennedy . Then another page. A letter from Betty Ford. On another, a long letter from Pat Nixon. Then a handwritten letter from Lady Bird Johnson. He points out with some disgust a printed message that says, "Hillary Rodham Clinton is much too busy . . . "

I'm dumbfounded. I look at Sumner. He laughs. "Someday I'll write a book about them all," he says. "I got to thinking one day about how sad it must have been for Mrs. Nixon being in the White House one day, and in disgrace and out the next, and living in exile, sort of, you know, in New Jersey. What was it like, and all—the loneliness, the pain? How do you get on with your life? I thought I knew something about all that since I had been cooped up here pretty much all my life on this island in this lighthouse, which my grandfather tended, and then my father for a while, until they put them all on computers, and I've spent a lot of hours in a ship's bunk at sea, and I thought maybe we had something in common, those ladies out of the limelight and I, and so I wrote to them, and they began writing back.

I would send them poems, you know, or little ideas, or funny things that happened here, and they would sometimes tell me a few things, and eventually I let them know I was writing to everybody and some of them were curious and I would mention what Nancy Reagan said about moving back to California or what Margaret Truman told me of her mother's place in Independence. I hear from Julie Nixon Eisenhower a lot too. She's very bright and articulate. I told her that in writing to her I was killing two birds with one stone. She liked that. She said her mother used to look forward to my letters. I was really sad to see Pat Nixon go. Few people made any effort to understand her. I think it was Gloria Steinem who did her in. I'm trying to get Barbara Bush up here now. I told her, 'Get George to sail his boat up this way for a change. I can put him on to bluefish or lobsters, whichever he wants.' Her secretary said she might."

When I leave Sumner's lighthouse, I know I've cracked his secret at last. I realize his light blinks out for lonely ladies and that the only fire he'll ever put out is the one in his generous soul. I decide his place gives out a lovely light. I know one day a boat will pull in and a passel of secret service men will shout out to Sumner, "He's coming, he's coming!" And I'll bet dollars to doughnuts Barbara Bush will be in the bow of the ship waving her crazy heart out like Joan of Arc of the Atlantic Ocean.

AUSTRIA NOON

Austria Noon invited me over to dinner at her place and like a fool I said yes. She practically begged me. "Patrick, I'm counting on you," she said. I didn't want to hurt her feelings, but she never really has gotten the message that I don't like Mozart, I don't think Dr. Samuel Johnson is funny, and I can't stand the three cats she has that reek up her house and get hairs in the cheese dip and all. I don't know whether Austria doesn't realize I strongly object to these things or whether she just doesn't see. She's always adjusting those glasses that slide down her nose. Once she told me she thought she looked like Edith Sitwell as painted by Hans Holbein. God!

Actually, I shouldn't be so hard on her. She is a very interesting person, no question of that. My job at the library is made much more enjoyable by her presence. She cracks jokes and makes faces during the most routine, boring tasks we are forced to do, so her sense of the incongruity of people like us slaving away in that archival dungeon is a great plus to me. But I'd like to keep it at that and not get too friendly, although she seems not to notice this in me or else she just plans to sweep it all aside, as she sometimes does, with over-alarming gusto. So I just wait and watch. That's sometimes my chief role in life.

There aren't many romances among the locals on Spanish Island. People generally go over to the mainland and off to Boston or Bangor for that. And certainly the public library is hardly an appropriate setting, despite Erich Segal. We are the one bastion of creativity against all the lobster-headed puritans that inhabit this place. Austria and I, to be truthful, regard ourselves as the only real intellectuals stationed on this lonely outpost all through the year--Winter Wet, Winter Cold, Mud Slop, and Tourists, which are our four primary seasons.

I got stuck here after I got back from Wales where I was living with my father. I had to take off a year before beginning graduate work in California. I plan to become a filmmaker and interpret all the days of my life and everybody else's in rich imagery like Federico Fellini. He is my favorite filmmaker. All my flicks will end with parties on the beach near water at dawn, just like his movies. Austria is jealous everytime I talk about Giulietta Massina. God, how Giulietta's pie face haunts me! Austria doesn't look anything like her. She looks more like a young Katharine Hepburn--a rag, a bone, and a hank of hair--a regular New England coatrack, if you ask me. That's fine, too, but Austria has a motor mouth, just like the Great Kate, with opinions on every subject, including what I should do with my life and whom I should spend it with, and she doesn't seem to give one damn about my feelings or ideas on any of this. Which is why I have to be careful about accepting dinner invitations from her. I can't have her landing on first base with me.

It was my mother's idea that I should take this job at the library for the whole year. She assured me time would go fast, but sometimes I feel as though I've been sentenced to death. The only consolation I get is a meager pittance for my work, but what can you spend it on here? It's an hour over to Port Clyde or East Harmony and neither is exactly Hong Kong-on-the-Penobscot, is it? Wait till I get to California! All hell will break loose out there, I guess. Maybe I'll have to make films in the florid Ken Russell style instead, for the first few years at least.

Austria's favorite opera is Mozart's *Don Giovanni*. She says it is her Jessie L. Weston that unlocks the secret to her whole *oeuvre*, whatever that may be. Personally, I think she got the whole *Don Giovanni* idea from that pimp George

Bernard Shaw, another British smartass she is forever quoting. "Heaven is Reality," she is always parroting to me at the library. "We should be so grateful that we have our Duties and Responsibilities to look forward to every day." Once when I devoured a second Hershey bar with almonds at lunch, she said to me in that lofty way of hers, "Patrick, Hell is Self-Indulgence. You should know that." Why should I be made to feel guilty all the time is what I want to know? Thanks, George, for all your help!

She thinks very little of the Welsh, too, even though she knows my father lives there. London is all she talks about. "The person who is tired of London is tired of life, Patrick," she reminds me, quoting that old fart Johnson again. "'For there is in London all that life can afford.' You should know that, Patrick." Yes, I know that, and I have heard New Yorkers say that about their city and people from Paris and San Francisco, and I say I'll take Rome and Los Angeles any day. But what do they know? They obviously will never make films. They probably have never even heard of the great Lindsay Anderson or Stanley Kubrick.

Another problem is that I am twenty-three years old. Austria Noon could be thirty or worse. Her father was some kind of doctor, a psychiatrist, I think, who came to Boston from London and did something at Harvard Medical, lectured, or was a professor, and they came up here to Spanish Island as summer people, the same way as my family originally did. The Noons were high-and-mighty people when we were young. They had people in for English teas when everybody else just broke out the beer and clams. Harpo, Jenny, and I didn't really play with Austria when we were little. She and her sister, Corinna, used to watch us from a distance, holding on to the protective posts of their family porch like fugitives from a Bronte novel. We were too rowdy for them, and too young, I am sure.

When we grew up, I went off to Dartmouth for college, but Austria, I think, went to Bryn Mawr or Radcliffe, someplace very spiffy and stiff. My mother said at one point that Austria had grown into such a lovely girl, but I paid no attention. Then, after my mother divorced my father, my mother moved into our summer house permanently, and I went off to Wales to pacify Dad and then came back here to stay with my mother. She is feeling very lost, I think. Jenny is married and lives in Connecticut. Harpo is a freshman at Dartmouth and off to France this summer on the Experiment in International Living. So I took this lackey job at the library when what to my wondering eyes should appear but Austria Noon, marooned here on the island two years since both her parents died. She just kind of preempted me into her prime time. I can tell you exactly what she will serve at dinner tonight. We will begin with Amontillado sherry and canapés with those awful salty anchovies curled up on them. Then will come consommé, heavily laced with sherry (she got that from Julia Child), then that terrible Boston scrod baked with little mushrooms or tiny shrimp rolling around in a cream sauce on top. Dessert will be two pieces of pound cake with Robertson's lemon curd spread between the layers like peanut butter. This is Austria's own concoction. Anything remotely British is always just perfect for her.

"Patrick," says Austria to me. "Have some more of that June Allyson stew. I can tell you really like it."

"Thanks," I say, sopping up some juice with my French bread. "You surprised me with this dish."

"That was intentional," she replies. "I know you love the "Industry," as you term movie-making, so I wanted to make something suitably thematic for you."

"It's really good," I say greedily, as she pours me a generous second. Boy, did she ever fake me out on this one!

"June Allyson used to cook this for her husband, Dick Powell. She would make up vats of it and store it on board their boat. Dick Powell requested this stew at least four nights a week."

"How do you know all this?" I ask. Is she Louella Parsons reincarnated?

"Research," she says. " I'm surprised at you, Patrick. Haven't you noticed there's a section called *Cooking* in our library?"

"Best stew I ever ate," I proclaim. "Fantastic aroma. What's the secret?"

"Tarragon and oregano in equal proportions. But don't eat too much. For dessert we're having Jill Clayburgh's Eat-Your-Heart-Out Chocolate Cheesecake."

"Ye gods," I say admiringly.

"So pleased you are so pleased," says Austria, grinning her giraffe smile and knocking her glasses back up her nose. I like the look of mirth breaking out in her eyes. I begin to think differently about Austria Noon.

Austria and I have entered into an agreement as the only two working intellectuals on Spanish Island. Monday evenings we meet at her house for dinner and readings. She is reading aloud Boswell's *Journal of a Tour in the Hebrides with Samuel Johnson, LL.D.* So far we have gotten to the Isle of Skye and are staying with Boswell and Dr. Johnson in a hotel in Portree. Dr. Johnson doesn't much like anything. Boswell is hyping everything desperately, of course, being a Scotsman.

Austria uses a gruff voice when she speaks as Johnson. It occurs to me that Dr. Johnson may be her father metamorphosed.

"Did your father talk like that?" I ask.

"My father?" asks Austria. "Why, no, I don't think so. What a strange thing to say!"

"You read the part so convincingly," I say. "As though you know this person well."

"I do," Austria says. "But not because I think he's my father. My father was a doctor. He never had opinions on anything, even life or death. I like Dr. Johnson because he is open, honest. He says exactly what he thinks, popularity be damned."

"Do you agree with what he says, though?" This is a test question.

"No, not always. But I admire forthrightness, his especially."

"He told Boswell that the two students who were expelled from Oxford for being Methodists deserved their fate because they had no business being Methodists."

"I know. Of course I don't agree with him there. He says the same thing about Quakers and anyone who isn't high church Tory Anglican, like him, but I don't know that he really is that insensitive, if you press him about it."

"Austria," I say. "The eighteenth century may be all right for you, but I prefer the twentieth."

"I don't see you in this century at all," replies Austria. "You seem much more a man of the sixteenth century, Patrick."

"Why?" I ask, astonished.

"Your film script," she says. "You don't think those inter-galactic fantasies you write belong in this century, do you? They are surreal, picaresque voyages and discoveries. I think you really are Magellan or Vasco da Gama, Patrick."

"Leonardo da Vinci," I say. "Please. If I must be from that period."

"Leonardo," she smiles. "We'll talk about it on Thursday at your house. What are you planning for dinner?"

"Welsh rarebit," I reply. "Done with beer. And a green salad. Is that all right?"

"That'll be fine, Patrick," says Austria, closing her book and sighing at me as though I'm hopeless.

My place. Thursday evening. Seven o'clock. My mother is in Connecticut for the week, thank God. I don't use the dining room, but set our places in the breakfast nook instead. I have three cookbooks in front of me—*The Gold Cook Book* by Louis De Gouy, *The Joy of Cooking* by Irma Rombauer, and *The Spanish Island Congregational Church Ladies' Society Receipts*. The last one is no help to me, even if it does have three recipes by my mother in it. Irma and Louis both have Welsh rarebit made with beer. Irma's recipe is better, I think, so she wins this time. I am using some New York sharp cheddar cheese instead of that Vermont stuff Old Sims carries in his store. Anything with "New York" in it is anathema to Old Sims. He's got a Hieronymous Bosch view of New York, I'm afraid, and has avoided going there all his life, just as he thinks he's avoided Hell, which is where he's going to end up anyway, I'm convinced, for all his provincial mean-spiritedness.

Austria arrives on time. We have an easy light-hearted dinner. Austria cracks me up imitating our boss, Mary Ellen Osborn, librarian *extraordinaire*, who wraps books in plastic anytime it looks like rain, as though the books were her own precious children. One day she even saw Mary Ellen demonstrating to a woman how to cradle books in her arms against the wind and weather.

I am surprised that Austria is drinking her beer from the can. I chilled a hollow stem glass for her, but, no, she is chugging away at it from the can, just like one of the locals.

"Let's get to your script—*The New Viridiana*,," she says as soon as we finish our dinner. "We were at a banquet at the launching site where all those people were celebrating the launching of that super satellite. Were those people Venusians?" she asks.

"We don't really know," I say. "I haven't indicated yet."

"There was a strangeness about the way they walked and talked," Austria says. "I thought they had to be Venusians or else some sort of aquatic beings stranded on the beach."

"They could be," I say. "Do you think I should be more explicit this early?"

"Well, I don't know," she says. "Read on and let's see."

What "we" see hits me like a small warning jolt from Austria: "There is no advantage in being mystifying, Patrick. You've got to indicate where you're coming from."

"Meaning what?" I ask, well aware that the topic has switched dangerously from my screenplay to me.

Austria looks at me. She reaches up her hands to turn my embarrassed face so that I have to look straight into her eyes. "Help me, God," I silently pray.

"Do you like me, Patrick?" she says. You could have knocked me over.

"Yes," I say, but it sounds very far away and I'm afraid this may mean more than I want it to mean.

She seems pleased. She drops her hands and laughs. "Well, good. That's a start. That's all I ask for, really, to be liked by you."

"We're good friends, aren't we?" I ask, on my guard.

"Maybe more than that," she says in a slight rush that starts a shiver down my back. "Haven't you ever thought . . ?"

"I'm leaving the end of August," I say, warning her.

"I know," she says, searching my face a little, making me turn away from what I see in her eyes. Then she gets up. "Well, I should be going. I hate to have you leave this island, Patrick," she adds.

"I've got to get on with it," I say. "My future is in California, not here. But I'll be back from time to time."

"Sure," she says. "See you tomorrow at the factory. Thanks. Think about that script. You want to complete the first draft before you leave, don't you?"

"Yes," I say. "See you tomorrow. Thanks for the advice."

I stand there watching her depart. I find my mind wondering about Austria and worrying about her, for some unknown reason. I know what she was saying and I'm afraid I may have hurt her feelings. I didn't mean to, but I never thought about her romantically until tonight. I actually think she really likes me. Odd that I should like her too, I mean, so much more than I used to. She has this sweet ineffable sadness sitting in her eyes that makes me want to put my arm around her and steady her for some reason. I don't think it's purely literary, although that has been the tie that binds us. Oh, God, what's got its hooks into me now? Doesn't she know that I have to take first things first? I must get through graduate school. I definitely need some kind of solid identity. I think life should be as orderly as possible. It bothers me when something crashes in to disturb a plan I'm working on. Damn Austria Noon! Why does she throw me into this dumb befuddlement? What will I say when I see her tomorrow? What will I reveal when she looks into my eyes? How will I ever get to California now?

I watch Austria walk down the road. She really almost dances, her personal choreography intimate, intricate, and entirely appealing. I follow her progress through the dark blue night, noticing that the street light down the road causes her angular figure to cast a huge shadow. I watch her figure get smaller and smaller, until, suddenly, I panic. I'm afraid she'll disappear forever. I run after her. "Hey, Austria," I call. "Wait up. I'll walk you home! I've got a whole new ending I want to tell you about!"

THE WINDS OF MARCH

We wrapped on Saturday, I was out of the bungalow at the Chateau in an hour, Dusty picked me up at ten, we got to LAX in half an hour, he caught his plane to London and I grabbed the Red Eye to New York via Dallas-Ft. Worth at a little after midnight. The best sleep I'd had in a month. And still there was JFK and Logan to come and then the long drive up from Boston to Port Clyde, always an amazing time warp for me, like rolling back my soul to the Middle Ages, or the Celtic Twilight, I suppose, in my case. Fishing boats, lobster traps, shacks—what are these? Do we light them with Fresnels or Lekos? Can they cheat this way a little, counter to the left for that medium shot? Pan the whole coast of Maine, will you? Now, give me a tight shot on a clam, will you? I like that little smile. Pan to that chorus line of oysters on the right. Voiceover: "And answer came there none." Music up. Helicopter shot: church steeple on a verdant island. Funeral procession.

I thought about her all the way. How long ago? Almost two months ago, just as we had begun shooting. Luckily, the director rescheduled my scenes. Renee was a help, playing the understanding angel. "Yeah, it's not like we all don't got mothers," Renee said to me, in her mock tough New York way. What an agent! The Heart of old Hollywood, I'd say. If even genuine feeling can be pitched, Renee will do it. But that's the bounty tag of the industry. Well, she got me in with Ovitz at C.A.A., and who's in that new flick with Costner, but Yours Truly; maybe it will work, maybe not, but *The Natural* didn't hurt and the part's bigger this time.

Why do I feel so guilty, then? Why do I feel as if I am betraying the whole family? Maybe because I couldn't make it to Boston on time. I tried. She knew I was coming, but, when I arrived, she was gone. Just like that. Eighty-five years old and evaporated in an afternoon, such a gallant old lady, the mixture of Scottish and Irish blood in her fighting, raging all the way to the end. And now, only Jenny and I left to settle the estate, no Harpo, our little brother, no mother, no father, just Jenny in Connecticut, and I in the air, "making my entrance again with my usual flair," a second-rate film player in his thirties hanging on to his youthful athleticism and his arguable charm. Not a director yet, not a leading actor, nothing to write home about, a Maine Yankee who should have known better. I can just hear the Spanish Islanders yapping about it. "Why'd anybody want to go out to California? Everybody knows Fred Allen said the only thing that thrives there is an orange." Even I know that Gloria Swanson said, when she moved back to New York from California, that "all that sun can't possibly be good for the brain." Addled, that's what I've become. Too much 72 Market Street, Spago, Polo Lounge, and Malibu. Put me on your menu and call me Avocado Delight. AVOCADO DELIGHT starring in FARCE: MY FORTE, I FEAR.

"Spanish Island, here I come. Right back where I started from." Reverse shot. Roll it. Show me backing up to Logan Airport in a 747 and getting on! "And now, folks, here comes Mr. Patrick Curtis, Avocado Delight, arriving in his Cutlass Ciera, courtesy of Hertz, at luxurious, swanky Port Clyde, Maine. Let's put him on the ferry and send him over to exotic, exciting Spanish Island. Mr. Curtis, I know it's foggy out today, but you have such a great tan. Could we ask you a few questions about your humble origins on our fair isle? Do you really think it will become another playground for The Rich and Famous? Is it true that Ally Sheedy, Liza Minelli, Debra Winger, and Mary Stuart Masterson are all flying in to meet you here?"

Cold, damp, mouldy wood, creosote, gull shit, gull cries, dull clang of unseen bell buoys, bass voice of foghorn. No one on deck except me, Captain California becoming Patrick Curtis, a young kid with a future.

"Sail on through the fog, sail on, sail on, and you'll never sail alone."

Wouldn't you know? They did film *Carousel* in Maine!

We pulled into the slip right on time. The boat chugged against the side, the ancient wood shrieked a couple of times and then surrendered.

"Jesus, Mary, and Ralph," said Ben, catching me roughly by the arm as I stepped off the boat. "What are you doing here this time of the year?"

"Thought I'd come out to check on the place."

"Seen you in that picture with Meryl Streep. How do you like being one of them men that paint their faces up like women and prance around on the screen?"

"Did you like the film?"

"Nope. Couldn't figure out what in the hell was going on. Why was she fooling around in Africa with that aviator. Does she really talk like that?

"No, she's an actress."

"So I heard tell. Heard she went to Vassar, also. Mrs. Alling went to Vassar, too. She don't talk like that. Your mother went to Vassar, didn't she?"

"That's right."

"She didn't talk like that. Sorry to hear about her, by the way."

"Yeah."

"She'll be missed this summer. Services down in Boston, were they?"

"Cambridge. Mt. Auburn."

"Your sister show up?"

"Yes, of course."

"Haven't seen her in three, maybe five years."

"No. She lives in Connecticut, you know."

"I know that. Haven't seen her here summers."

"Her husband's from Long Island. They go there."

"Don't say? I suppose that's bigger than us."

"Ben, the whole world is bigger than Spanish Island."

"Well, we got Deer Isle and Mt. Desert up here in Maine. Is Long Island bigger than those?"

"I guess so. Is the store open?"

"Maybe yes, maybe no. Can't tell. Depends on Sim's whims, we say around here. Well, I see a light on there. Let's go on up."

"No. I'll go round to the house first. I'll meet you there later."

"Suit yourself. You got till four o'clock. You don't mean to spend the night, do you?"

"I have to get back. I'll take the four o'clock boat."

"Suit yourself. Mrs. Hamilton could put you up, you know."

"Thanks. I have just this one afternoon. I have to get back to Boston and then back to the Coast. I'm starting this new movie with Kevin Costner."

"Never heard of him. The Coast, is it? Thought you were on the coast right here."

"Touché. This is the real coast."

"You bet your ass it is."

The mud season. Nothing romantic about this place. Cold, grey, moody sky. Gulls screaming, bell buoys straining and clanging in the water. Wooden boards like little gangplanks, over the pools of water and mud, leading you up to the front doors of houses. Unpleasant little splashes lapping at one's ankles. The smell of cracked clams on the rocks stinking up the air. Only the ferryboat tied up at the wharf. I was the sole passenger over from the mainland to this island, the one thing in my life that seemed immutable up to now.

You don't tell your troubles to anyone on this island. You don't tell anything to anyone on this island. Everything is kept locked in. Humor is rare; confidences rarer. We are in the hands of a cold, cynical god here. Nothing is given easily, and everything can be taken away swiftly. There is no such thing as mercy, only a relentless push toward something, an urge to hang on, to turn oneself into a creature that develops a hard shell that cannot be scraped off, something very much like a barnacle, like Ben Whitefield, who must be in his sixties now and has been ferrying people and cars over from the mainland since he was a young kid. I worked with him one summer when I was sixteen. I think he had to be born out of the sea somewhere, a human crustacean— huge brown hands with capable tentacles that become ropes, knots, cables, lifelines at will.

I grew up on this island. I spent summers here, and then, after my parents' divorce, whole years of my life. I went to school here. I learned to sail here, to swim, to envy the jaunty summer visitors who came every July and August and opened their houses, decked them out in petunias and geraniums, and had slews of friends in for laughter and parties. And I watched them depart and helped them onto the ferryboat with martinis in their hands and waved goodbye to them when the summer sun went down and the season was over. And finally I joined them. I just didn't want to stay put.

My mother loved this house. It's a lot weather-beaten, silver-grey, just like her. When the winds of March whip around it, as they are doing today, the old house creaks and groans, protesting against the agonies of nature. You can hear it if you listen. That's just the way my mother went, according to Jenny's account, dying there in the hospital in Boston. Jenny said that in her final hour she had her head turned toward the window with her arm stretched out. What was she reaching for, I wonder? This house? This creaking wooden house of security which she inherited from her father and now has passed on to me?

What will I do with it? How does it fit into my life now? My life as an actor seems all wrong, purposeless, ill-suited to the person I was when I was here. That young man is gone now. What I know of sunshine and camellias and fashionable Beverly Hills villas with sunken pools would strike me down dead in my tracks among these people on this island. I was always a summer person to them, anyway. I never really belonged. You can see this in Ben's eyes. He sees me as a soft, spoiled rich kid who sold out and does nothing decent for a living. And he's right, from the Spanish Island point of view.

Well, the house has memories, but they no longer are my memories. I cast a cold eye on the old house now, like a ruthless real estate appraiser. That front door needs repair. Two screws have pulled out in that top hinge. That's dangerous. That white trim on the dining room window didn't winter well. Has to be painted. Someone left that screen on by mistake in my old bedroom upstairs. That pine's grown way too big down by the dock. Needs drastic pruning, I'd say.

My place and not my place. I can't get here summers. Jenny can't get here summers. She prefers East Hampton. My legacy, my inheritance, my problem now. Something wants me here, though. There's a hint of a crocus or two around the back door where my mother planted them long ago.

The store smells good. There's a fire in the woodburning stove. Old Sims says, "How do?" That's as effusive as he gets. He must be eighty-nine now, still pink-cheeked, pipe smoking, lumpish body moving like some impudent bear.

"How do, sir," I reply respectfully.

"Sorry she croaked," he says, offering me some coffee.

"Thank you, no," I say politely.

"How's tricks in Hollywood?" says Ben, laughing more than it deserves at the sub-text he puts into the remark.

"Hooray," I reply, making a ding-a-ling gesture in the air.

. "Can't believe a Vassar girl'd talk like that," says Ben.

"Who's that?" asks Sims.

"Name's Meryl Streep," Ben says. Sims looks puzzled. "Don't matter, Sims. You wouldn't know. You don't never go to the movies, do you?"

"Can't say as I do," says Sims.

"She's just an actress," I explain to Sims.

"Oh, I seen actresses all right," says Sims. "I went to Boston once. They had a place called the Old Howard." He and Ben laugh until Ben breaks out of it with a hacking cough.

"I'm catching the four o'clock boat back," I say to Sims.

"You bet you are," he says.

I pick up a package of gum. "I'll take some of this," I say.

"There you go," says Sims, ringing it up and giving me change. "Will you be coming this summer?"

"I'd like to," I say. "But I don't know."

"This man's in pictures," says Ben, putting his arm around my shoulder. This man's gonna be on the Jay Leno *Tonight* show one day."

Sims whistles. He's impressed, but he doesn't watch television either.

"Did you know Leno's from Boston, actually Andover?" says Ben. "If you see him, tell him to lay off those Bob Dole jokes he's still cracking. Makes it appear as though Leno's a God-damned liberal."

"Is Bob Dole that young pup who was running for President?" asks Sims.

"That's right," says Ben.

"Don't think much of him," says Sims. " I didn't vote for him."

"You voted for Clinton, didn't you?" Ben asks, surprised.

"Can't say as I did," says Sims, pushing up his glasses and smiling.

"You mean you voted for Perot?" says Ben.

"I'm still looking for a New Englander," says Sims. "Haven't had a good one since Kennedy. I didn't like Dukakis. Was Roosevelt from Boston?"

"No, but George Bush has got a big place down in Kennebunkport," I tell Sims.

"Summer resident," says Sims. "That man can't fish." He looks at me. "Sorry, Patrick. Didn't mean to offend."

"Come on," says Ben to me. "I'll walk you over to the ferry."

We walk pretty much in silence. We make a big thing out of watching the boat pull in. Ben wants to know if I ever met Dolly Parton. I board the ferry. Again, I am the only passenger going back.

"Real nice to see you, Pat. I'll keep my eye on the house for you."

"Thanks."

"Write if you get work." He roars with laughter and splutters into a cough again.

The boat pulls out. Ben gets smaller and smaller. I see him wave. A tiny voice calls out, "Say hello to Meryl Streep for me. Tell her to learn how to speak English."

I watch until all I can see is the island. Then it becomes a blue line in the distance. I turn my back and go inside the cabin. I think of a line I once had to say when I played Prince Hamlet at Dartmouth, "But break my heart, for I must hold my tongue." I know now that I will have to rent out the house to a succession of anonymous summer people until one day somebody will want to buy it and perhaps it will come alive again.

ON SPANISH ISLAND

32 Lett's Mill Road
Boody's Cove, Maine
January 20, 1996

Mr. Bill Anzalone
Anzalone's Mortuary
5031 Fremont Court Road
San Francisco, California

Dear Bill,

As I promised, I am writing to you after returning home from the American Morticians Society convention in Chicago, Illinois. I was grateful I took the Amtrak train since the weather was pretty chilly when I arrived in Boston. Hope that you, too, got home safely to San Francisco, although I heard the winter storms have been pretty severe out there this year.

As I told you in Chicago, my dad always said about our mutual trade that "when they come a-looking, we know they'll be a-buying."

Now you asked about Spanish Island, where I live, and since you asked me a lot of questions, I've been doing a lot of thinking, and I am wondering: Are you thinking of maybe coming here for a vacation (we don't call the State of Maine "Vacationland" for nothing, you know), or are you hankering on buying a piece of property or renting for the summer?

I know you can't be thinking of opening a rival mortuary here because the number of clients you would get can't begin to meet the opportunities you must have in San Francisco, especially with the frequency of those earthquakes and the constant threat of the Big One that is supposed to be heading your way someday soon. Of course, you do operate a crematorium, which I don't do, and you may have it in your head to update my business through competition which, if you intend to do so, I hope you will inform me openly and honestly, in the way you always discussed everything with me over drinks in Chicken-on-the-Car-and-the-Car-Won't-Go. Will you ever forget that waitress who served those margaritas to us? Was her name Frieda or Fritzie? I don't think I ever got it straight.

At any rate, here is a rundown on my part of the world. You don't have to send me anything about San Francisco. I know all about it. As I indicated to you in Chi-town, I'll match you view for view with my Spanish Island and I'll bet I'd come out the winner. I shall try to be as objective as I can be, giving you the bad as well as the good, some of the history as well as the present. For your part, will you write and let me know what you are up to? If it's to fish, or sail, or just for a nice visit, the wife and I will be glad to put you up for a week or so, which would give you a good opportunity to become acquainted with all the beauty we've got in this part of the world. Here goes:

Spanish Island lies in the cold Atlantic about fifteen miles off the coast of Maine. It is larger than Deer Isle, as picturesque as Monhegan Island, and, its permanent inhabitants maintain, as sophisticated as Martha's Vineyard or Nantucket in that bustling commonwealth to the south, Doowhatchachoosits.

Spanish Island gets its name because its earliest inhabitants were Portuguese fishermen who invented the myth that the island was the most eastern point of land in North America with no land coming between it and the Iberian peninsula. That's what they claimed, at any rate.

The early English inhabitants of the State of Maine didn't quarrel with that. They thought the island was the appropriate place for people who didn't speak English, anyway, and they clumsily called the whole place "Spanish Island " out of their superior ignorance. Besides, they thought the island was too far out and isolated to be good for anything except as a campground for aberrant Bostonians and New Yorkers who foolishly wanted to rough it in summer cottages that kept getting larger and more elaborate all the time, aping their neighbors to the north in stuck-up Seal Harbor and Bar Harbor.

To get to Spanish Island, one has to catch the ferry from Port Clyde or East Harmony. Service is pretty good, at least two trips out and back daily, year round, more in the summer when the tourists arrive.

Year round population on the island is almost 1500 hearty souls. In the summer, add 3000 more, plus more boats, animals, and automobiles.

It costs $30 to bring a car over to the island one way unless one has an annual permit, so a lot of people leave their cars on the mainland and walk when they get to the island. They haul little red wagons around with them wherever they go, looking like overgrown kids in a huge daycare playground.

There is only one gas station on the island, anyway, Nick's Sunoco in Boody's Cove, and one general store-post office presided over by Bennett Sims, 89 years old now, called "Old Sims" by the town boys and some of their parents. His store is known irreverently as Lower Yugoslavia because of its lack of supplies and Sims' steadfast refusal to order goods that move too fast. Sims is an old-liner who has set his face against progress. "Place is getting too big for its britches," says Sims, looking askance at what the mainlanders have accomplished. "I wouldn't give you a Spanish farthing for that Yuppieville called Portland," he says derisively.

Spanish Island is not flat and it's not all granite. It is about six miles long and two and a half miles wide. At its northern end, it rises up to imposing cliffs culminating in Diablo Point with a dangerous drop to a sandy beach down below called Bareass Beach by the local kids because if you can risk the treacherous tides there you don't really need to bother about a bathing suit.

In Boody's Cove, where most of the inhabitants live, there is a long wharf with the Port Clyde Ferry Office Building dominating it and a restaurant now called "The Shrimp Shack." Front Street, with its row of impressive captains' houses, some with widows' walks on top, a few antique shops, a glassblowing shop, and Mrs. Haines' large garden which is the island's unofficial botanical garden, runs along the harbor in the Cove.

Rising up from the water is a long hill called "Lighthouse Hill," crowned with an impressive green and white lighthouse at the top. The beacon still casts out its searching light every evening, and on foggy nights one can still hear its hoarse foghorn calling out to ghosts of mariners past and all who listen now.

Off to the right on the eastern crest of the hill is the elementary school and next to it the new cheap pink brick S. I. Junior High and High School, the construction of which brought about a major division in town between those who wanted to shuttle the older students over to the mainland as usual and those who wanted them to stay on the island.

The new brooms won, pointing out that our chief export was our young. Why should Massachusetts get the cream of Maine's crop? was the battle cry the winning side used, pointing out that there wasn't even a medical school in the whole state of Maine for a long time, meaning that one had to go out of state to get advanced training, and, some thought, even a decent general education.

The town cemetery, called the "Old Patten Cemetery," is up Lighthouse Hill Road also. The Pattens were the first of the farm families here back in the 19th century.

The Southern end of the island is taken up by Cobb's Point where early settlers like the Pattens and the Cobbs tried to make their living on saltwater farms, because the earth there was very fertile and the climate seemed warmed by the Gulf Stream and the southern exposure. These farms were bought up in the 1950s and 1960s by lawyers, doctors, and other business people who made them into comfortable second homes for themselves.

One old farm called "July Blue" has been in the hands of the Curtis family from Boston since 1907. At times, they have lived in the place year round. Jarvis Curtis was a Professor of Geology at Harvard for a few years before he went back to Wales to live permanently. His father, Henry Curtis, who was Welsh, was the man who bought "July Blue" from one of the Pattens who owned it. The main house was built around the turn of the century sometime. Of course, it has all been improved now, "be-gadgeted up," as Old Sims puts it.

The island has two churches--St. Anthony's Catholic Church and the Spanish Island Congregational Church. More people seem to go to St. Anthony's, but the Congo Church seems to have more clout in everything. They've got all that Boston Punitarian and Mayflower arrogance on their side.

Almost everybody attends the Citizens' Town Meeting held every year in September after Labor Day. The perennial complaint is always about the summer visitors. Too many of them, too noisy, and too lazy, people say.

The six-person Board of Selectmen includes Dr. Darrell Ashby, retired Judge from Boston, and Grace Hamilton, English-born owner of a Spanish Island Bed & Breakfast and former co-owner of The Shrimp Shack until her husband deserted her and ran away with a red-haired waitress named Ginny. That provided some talk for a long time, you can bet. Peter Coimbre, Barton Sims (Old Sims' son), Lula Martindale, and Ansel Sargent (best fisherman around) are the others on the current board.

Dr. Ashby is the most admired. People listen to what he says. He also represents one of only four black families in town, all of them highly respected and sought after by everybody.

Barton Sims and Lula Martindale, everyone agrees, are mostly hot air, predictably conservative and Republican on most issues. "Just plain selfish," is how Ansel Sargent puts it.

He is credited with having the most common sense and the best sense of humor. He owns a fleet of fishing boats for hire, most of which he keeps over in Boothbay Harbor.

Peter Coimbre is the youngest member and the town radical. Nothing ever seems right to him, but, although he complains a lot, he doesn't have too many alternative solutions to offer. Sometimes he seems cowed by his own family's Portuguese tradition. After all, the Coimbres have been on Spanish Island since the middle of the 19th century when it was first populated. The problem is that Peter just hasn't done as well as some of his ancestors. He's trying to run a printing press out of his home now, but Spanish Islanders don't have much to print. Peter doubles as Acquisitions Librarian at the town library, but that doesn't bring in too much business either.

There isn't much activity in the arts on the island, unfortunately, except in the summer when a few weekend artists arrive for one day at a time from the mainland. They like the way the light breaks here, they say.

Some families have had a few children who have taken to writing, painting, music, and even dancing. The Noon family was quite cultivated and genteel and gave the place a nice tone back in the 1960s.

Patrick Curtis was a sometime actor and director who was in a Meryl Streep film that nobody liked. Too long and too talky, everyone agreed.

Eleanor Loring gave piano lessons for a while and her husband sang in the Congo Church until they got fed up with our winters and moved to Santa Barbara, California.

Dickie Drummond is reported to be lead singer in a rock band somewhere in Massachusetts. Heard he wears his hair down to his shoulders and has a diamond earring in his ear. His grandmother was the featured attraction in our emporium last week--lovely woman, but Dickie never showed up. Sent a message he had a gig, which didn't surprise any of us.

Mrs. Phelps gives readings occasionally in the library. She's the President of the Spanish Island Literary Club and writes poems. People call her our Poet Laureate, but we're not inclined to believe everything we hear or read in print, no matter how much Mrs. Phelps may pipe up about it. That's about all there is of culture here.

The main industry really is tourism which comes easy as pie for Spanish Islanders. They don't have to do much about it. They just exist. People come to them and seem to like them the way they are. So the natives try to be accommodating and tolerant.

Apart from that, fishing and boat rentals are the other commercial industries. Shrimp and lobster are the big specialties, although they do put out boats after blues when they are running and Zinsser Brothers always lays up a good supply of cod, haddock, and scrod that keeps everybody happy.

There is one real doctor in town who keeps me informed when he spots a likely client for my business, but we also have two dentists and one periodontist. That's what Nancy Hillman calls herself. She and her husband David were both educated in Philadelphia and they have the snappiest office in town with Muzak any way you want it. With him as dentist and Nancy as periodontist, they've pulled a lot of business away from the other dentist, cranky Dr. Quatraro, who must be in his sixties now.

Good things about the island? I would say the air, first of all. We've got a lot of moisture and fog all the time. It's good for your skin. Cleanses your pores. Perspective is another. We're always looking to some far horizon. Makes your eyesight keener, your eyes bluer or browner. Dandy for what may lie behind them.

Self-sufficiency is another. We don't yammer when things go wrong. We just do it or fix it, whatever it is.

Appreciation is another. We really appreciate warm weather and sunlight when we get it, which truthfully is a lot of the time. Also, we don't need television with its constant six o'clock or eleven o'clock news. We don't believe that something newsworthy happens every single day. We reckon about once every two weeks something important like a war breaking out or an earthquake in Turkey should be called to our attention.

I think we're strongly individualistic, too. We may seem a lot alike on the outside and in what we do, but inside we're quite private and silent. Our interiors are all very different, and we prize that quality in others. We despise those nervous mainlanders who are just shells, people who can't sit still or shut up when they're supposed to. We take silence in our stride. In fact, we welcome it.

Bad points? Can't think of many.

Wish we had a good French restaurant in town, which we don't. Pleased that we don't have a McDonald's yet, although it's been thought of, but voted down, fortunately.

We all wish our taxes wouldn't keep going up all the time, but we blame that on the fools we regularly elect to represent us in Augusta.

Wish our high school graduates would win a few more prizes instead of losing out all the time to those Portland and Bangor con artists.

Wish our summer people wouldn't be so damn blasé every July and August and jump into the ocean when they've had too many martinis. Howard Pignola actually received a State of Maine citation for his courageous work in saving and reviving eight of them so far. *Downeast Magazine* did a damn good profile on Howard and our whole fire department as a tribute to his good work.

Personally, I think Spanish Island is a living poem.

I love our trees here and the roses, nasturtiums, and morning glories that crop up around our peeling white fences every summer.

I love the tart smell of the pines when you walk through them up near Cobb's Point.

I like the colors--chalky reds, yellows, blue-greys--that play over the face of the bluffs at Point Diablo on a day when the sky is full of frenzied, racing clouds.

I like the feel of the wind in my face and the spit of the spindrift on an autumn day when the ocean is roiling up for some sort of unpredictable stormy outburst.

And I like the feel of a boat underneath me, especially when one is sailing, and it's you being tested against the wind and sea. It's a struggle, maybe, but you know that there is a force straining inside you that makes you take on whatever Nature's got in store, and so you have to participate. You can't just sit back and wait. We don't ever do that on Spanish Island. We act. We work hard each day. We hatch plans each night.

Let me know when you are planning on coming.

Sincerely,

your friend,

Maurice Pelletier

Roger Lee Kenvin, a graduate of Bowdoin College in Maine with advanced degrees in English and Drama from Harvard and Yale, has lived and worked in Switzerland, England, and India, as well as in the United States. His short stories have been published in many literary periodicals.